The Wind in the
Willows
Country Cookbook

The Wind in the Willows
Country Cookbook

Inspired by
The Wind in the Willows
by Kenneth Grahame

Recipes by
ARABELLA BOXER

Illustrated by
ERNEST H. SHEPARD

CHARLES SCRIBNER'S SONS
NEW YORK

Library of Congress Cataloging in Publication Data
Boxer, Arabella, Lady.
  The wind in the willows country cookbook.
  Includes index.
Summary: Includes one hundred easy-to-follow recipes for a
variety of dishes, for all kinds of occasions, inspired by
characters and events in "The Wind in the Willows."
  1. Cookery, British. [1. Cookery, English] I. Shepard,
Ernest H. (Ernest Howard), 1879–1976, ill. · II. Grahame,
Kenneth, 1859–1932. Wind in the willows. III. Title.
TX717.B725 1983   641.5942   83-20073
ISBN 0-684-18000-6

1 3 5 7 9 11 13 15 17 19   Q/C   20 18 16 14 12 10 8 6 4 2

Printed in the United States of America.

Contents

1   FOOD FOR STAYING AT HOME

Eggy Bread*   2
Fried Marmalade Sandwiches*   2
Fried Cheese Sandwiches*   3
Sardines on Toast*   3
Mushrooms on Toast   4
Cinnamon Toast*   4
All-Bran Loaf   5
Scrambled Eggs with Tomato Puree*   6
Baked Eggs with Cheese and Ham*   7
Curried Eggs   8
Egg Salad*   9
Cauliflower Gratin   10
Toad-in-a-Bad-Hole*   11
Wayfarers' Easy Pizza   12
Macaroni Cheese   14
Fish Pie   15
Kedgeree*   16
Herrings in Oatmeal*   17
Smoked Haddock (or Cod) with Tomatoes*   18
Leek Pudding   19
Boiled Ham with Parsley Sauce   20
Potato Cake*   21
Bubble and Squeak*   22
Easy Banana Pudding*   22
Mixed Fruit Fool*   23
Pancakes   24
Jam Roly-Poly   26
Apple Snow*   27

2 FOOD FOR STAYING IN BED

Chicken Noodle Soup   30
Potato Soup*   32
Moly's Marmite Soldiers*   33
A Simple Rice Pudding*   34
Sliced Bananas in Orange Gelatin*   35
Milk Shake Ripple*   36
Eggnog   36
Honey and Lemon Drink*   38
Lemonade*   39
Lemonade II*   39

3 FOOD FOR THE STORAGE CUPBOARD

Ratty's Potted Meat*   42
Potted Fish*   43
Kipper Paste*   45
Marseilles Potted Shrimp*   46
Pickled Onions   47
Nutty Spice Island Mixture*   48
Tomato Chutney   49
By-ways Blackberry Jelly   50
Crab Apple Jelly   52
Plum Jam   54
Frozen Milky Way*   54
Chocolate Chip Cookies   55
Refrigerator Cookies   56

4 FOOD FOR EXCURSIONS

Riverside Sandwich*   60
Sausage Sandwich*   60
Potted Shrimp Sandwich*   61
Toad Hall Steak Sandwich*   61
Stuffed Eggs*   62
River-Banker's Lunch*   62
Hard-Cooked Eggs with Nutty Spice Island
    Mixture*   63
Sausage Rolls   64
Leafy Summer Lettuce Snacks*   66

Cornish Pasties   67
Hot Meat Pasties   68
Rabbit Pasties   70
Easy Meat Loaf *   72
Very Easy Flapjacks*   74
Flapjacks*   75

5   FOOD FOR CELEBRATIONS

Cauliflower, Egg, and Shrimp Mayonnaise*   78
Eggs in Onion Sauce   79
Raw Vegetables with Dipping Sauce*   80
Veal Stroganoff   81
Red Lion Spare Ribs with Barbecue Sauce   82
River-Banker's Broiled Chicken*   83
Chicken Pie   84
Steak and Kidney Pie   86
Game Pie   88
Salmon Fish Cakes*   90
Potato Puree*   91
Snowfalls in Dark Woods   92
Millionaire's Bread and Butter Pudding   93
Apples with Chocolate*   94
Baked Bananas*   94
Cheesecake *   95
Toad Hall Trifle   96
Plum Crumble*   98
Blackberry and Apple Meringue   98
Pebbles in a Stream   99
Floating Islands   100
Frozen Strawberry Fool*   101
Buried Strawberries *   102
Vanilla Ice Cream   102
Pearly Dawn Sorbet*   103
Nut Grove Ice Cream   104
Raspberry Sauce*   106
Melted Milky Way Sauce *   106
Oh My! Toffee Sauce*   107
Hot Chocolate Sauce*   107

Drop Cookies* 108
Bottled Sunshine Orange Cakes 109
Small Chocolate Cakes 110
Plum Cake 111
Carrot Cake* 112

INDEX 115

Recipes marked with a star * are easy to make

The Wind in the
Willows
Country Cookbook

1
Food for
Staying at Home

These are fairly simple things, good for making for yourself
and a couple of friends, or just for yourself when you are
alone and feeling hungry. Some of the recipes are for
proper cooked meals, such as Cauliflower Gratin; others are
for snacks, such as Cinnamon Toast. They can all be made
by hand, although some are quicker and easier to make if
you have the use of a blender or food processor.

Eggy Bread

2 eggs
Thickly sliced white bread,
    1–2 days old
2 tablespoons (30 g) butter
    plus 2 tablespoons
    vegetable oil
or 3 tablespoons (45 g) butter

Optional extras:
Fried bacon
or
Sugar
4 tablespoons (60 ml) syrup
Juice of ½ lemon

Draining on
absorbent paper
improves most
fried foods

Beat the eggs. Cut the crusts off the bread slices and dip
each slice in beaten egg, allowing excess egg to drain back
into the dish. Heat the butter and oil in a frying pan or
skillet over medium heat; you can use all butter if you
prefer. Fry the eggy bread until golden on each side. Drain
for a moment on paper towels, then lay on a hot dish.
Serve, either with strips of bacon for breakfast or supper, or
sprinkled with sugar and accompanied by a sauce of syrup
warmed with lemon juice as a dessert, or with syrup, for tea.

Fried Marmalade Sandwiches

Serves 3–4
6 slices stale white bread
Butter

Marmalade

The butter should
be taken out of the
refrigerator an hour
before starting

Butter the bread and spread half the slices with marmalade.
Make into sandwiches and cut off the crusts. Cut each
sandwich into 4 small squares, pressing them together
lightly. Heat some butter in a frying pan or skillet over
medium heat until very hot but not yet smoking. Put in
some of the little sandwiches, being careful not to crowd
them, and fry until golden brown on each side, turning
once. Drain on paper towels while you fry the rest, then
serve immediately. These are good for tea, or as a dessert;
for a special meal, serve with a bowl of whipped cream.

Fried Cheese Sandwiches

Serves 2

4 slices dry white bread	2 ounces (55 g) Cheddar
Butter	cheese

Remember that butter on its own can quickly overheat and burn

Spread the bread with butter. Cut the cheese in very thin slices, and divide it between 2 of the slices. Cover with the remaining bread to make 2 sandwiches, pressing them together. Then cut off the crusts. Melt 2 tablespoons (15 g) butter in a large frying pan or skillet. (An electric frying pan is good for this dish.) When it is hot, but not yet smoking, put in the sandwiches, cover the pan, and cook for about 2 minutes. Turn them over and cook for another 2 minutes. When they are crisp and golden on both sides, drain for a moment on paper towels; then serve on warmed plates.

Sardines on Toast

Serves 2

1 (4⅜-ounce/125 g) can sardines in oil	2 slices bread
	A little butter

Preheat the broiler. Open the can of sardines carefully and drain off the oil. Toast the bread lightly, then cut off the crusts and spread thinly with butter. Divide the sardines between the 2 pieces of toast, laying them head to tail. Put under the broiler for 3–4 minutes, gently warming them through. (If possible, have the broiler turned down low, or have the pan some distance away from it.) Enough for 2 as a snack or light meal.

The result was not so very depressing after all, though of course it might have been better; a tin of sardines—a box of captain's biscuits, nearly full—and a German sausage encased in silver paper.

Mushrooms on Toast

Serves 4

8 ounces (225 g) small
   mushrooms
5 tablespoons (75 g) butter
1 tablespoon all-purpose flour
1¼ cups (300 ml) milk

4 tablespoons heavy cream
Salt and freshly ground
   black pepper to taste
4 thick slices stale bread

It is always wise to wear an apron when cooking

Wipe the mushrooms and cut off the stems. Slice the stems and leave the caps whole. Heat 3 tablespoons (45 g) butter in a frying pan or skillet and cook the mushrooms over low heat until soft. Lift them out of the pan, reserving the juices, and chop them coarsely. Melt the remaining 2 tablespoons (30 g) butter in a small saucepan over low heat and stir in the flour. Cook gently for 1 minute, stirring. Meantime, heat the milk in another pan; pour on the hot milk. Stir until blended. Then add the juices from the frying pan, the cream, and salt and pepper to taste. Cook gently for 3 minutes. Then put in the chopped mushrooms and keep warm while you toast the bread. Lay it on warmed plates and pour the mushrooms over. Serve immediately. This makes a good hot dish for a lunch or light supper.

Cinnamon Toast

Serves 2–3

2 tablespoons sugar
½ teaspoon cinnamon

4 slices stale white bread
Butter

Preheat the broiler. Mix the sugar and cinnamon in a small bowl. Toast the bread lightly, then cut off the crusts. Spread with butter and sprinkle thickly with the cinnamon and sugar mixture. Put under the broiler until the sugar has melted and turned golden brown. Cut each slice into 3 strips and serve immediately, on a warmed plate. This is good eaten at teatime.

Melted sugar should be watched carefully, as it can quickly turn from being golden brown to being burned

All-Bran Loaf

A suitable pan should be taken out and prepared before starting

Makes 1 loaf
Butter
1 cup (120 g) All-Bran
½ cup (120 g) light brown sugar
10 ounces (275 g) currants or raisins, or mixed dried fruit
1¼ cups (300 ml) milk
¾ cup (120 g) self-rising flour

First choose your loaf pan; This will measure roughly 7 × 4 × 3½ inches (18 × 10 × 8.5 cm). Rub it all over inside with softened butter.

Preheat the oven to 350° F (175° C). Then mix the All-Bran, sugar, and dried fruit in a large bowl, using your hands. When they are well mixed, add the milk slowly, stirring with a wooden spoon. Leave for 30 minutes, then sift the flour into the mixture, stirring again until all is blended. Tip it into the greased pan and bake in the oven for 1¼ hours. When done, take it completely out of the pan and set on a rack to cool. Wait until it is quite cool—about 1½ hours—before eating, or it may give you a pain! Cut in thick slices and spread with butter.

The following morning Toad, who had overslept himself as usual, came down to breakfast disgracefully late, and found on the table a certain quantity of egg-shells, some fragments of cold and leathery toast, a coffee-pot three-fourths empty, and really very little else; which did not tend to improve his temper, considering that, after all, it was his own house.

Scrambled Eggs with Tomato Puree

4 large eggs
Salt and freshly ground black pepper to taste
3 tablespoons (45 g) butter
2 thick slices whole wheat bread
1 tablespoon canned tomato puree

Scrambled eggs do not improve by being kept hot

Break the eggs into a bowl and beat lightly, until the yolks and whites are just blended without being smoothly mixed. Add a pinch of salt and a few twists of the pepper mill. Put the bread in the toaster and warm a thick pan; it can be a frying pan or small saucepan, but a sauté pan with rounded edges is best of all. Drop in half the butter. Give the eggs another quick beating, and as soon as the butter has melted, pour them in. Start stirring gently once the eggs are in the pan. I like to use an old silver spoon for making scrambled eggs, for I find the sharp edge good for scraping the eggs off the bottom of the pan. Most people use a wooden spoon, but you may find a metal spoon easier, as I do. As the eggs start to thicken, start scraping the curds of egg from the bottom of the pan, especially in the center, where they cook first. The whole process should be slow and gradual, unlike making an omelette, which must be done very quickly. Scrape the bottom of the pan slowly and rythmically, allowing quite large curds to form before lifting them gently and allowing the liquid egg to run underneath. Before the eggs have all set, remove the pan from the heat and prepare the toast. Spread each slice first with some of the remaining butter and then with tomato puree, and lay on hot plates. The eggs will have thickened slightly by now, for they go on cooking in the heat of the pan. Give them a final stir and replace over the heat for a moment if they are not quite cooked enough. They should be soft and firm, moist rather than dry and solid. Spoon onto the toast and eat right away. This is good with a green salad.

Baked Eggs with Cheese and Ham

Do make sure that the baked eggs are not allowed to overcook, as they will become rubbery

Serves 3–4

Butter

About 6–8 thin slices bread (2 per person)

About 6 ounces (175 g) sliced ham

5 ounces (150 g) Cheddar cheese

Freshly ground black pepper

6–8 eggs (2 per person)

Preheat the oven to 350° F (175° C). Rub a large shallow baking dish or baking pan with butter. Cut the crusts off the bread, butter the slices, and lay them, overlapping, in the dish. Trim most of the fat off the ham and lay the ham over the bread. Slice the cheese and lay it over the ham, sprinkling with black pepper. Break the eggs carefully over the cheese and bake until the whites are just set. This may take anywhere from 15 to 30 minutes, depending on the size and thickness of the dish, and of the layers of bread, ham, and cheese. Serve as a main dish, with a green salad.

Rat, warm and comfortable, dozed by his fireside. His paper of half-finished verses slipped from his knee, his head fell back, his mouth opened, and he wandered by the verdant banks of dream rivers.

Curried Eggs

Serves 4

8 eggs
1 large bunch scallions, *or* 1 medium onion, *or* 1 leek
4 tablespoons (60 g) butter
1½ tablespoons all-purpose flour
½ tablespoon ground coriander *or* 1 tablespoon curry powder

½ tablespoon ground cumin
1¼ cups (300 ml) chicken stock
½ cup plus 2 tablespoons (150 ml) light cream
Salt and black pepper to taste

To ensure that the egg yolks are perfectly centered, turn the eggs over halfway through the cooking time

Hard-cook the eggs for 12 minutes, then leave in cold water for a few minutes while you prepare the sauce. If using scallions, keep the white parts and the best green leaves separate. Slice the white parts and chop the leaves. If using an ordinary onion, cut it in half and then slice each half thinly. If using a leek, cut it in half lengthwise, wash well, and cut each half in semicircular slices. Heat the butter in a pan over medium heat and cook the white parts of the scallion, or the sliced onion or leek, for 2 minutes. Add the flour, coriander, or curry powder, and cumin and cook for another 2 minutes, stirring slowly all the time. Heat the stock and cream together without allowing to reach boiling point; pour onto the curry mixture slowly, stirring until all is smoothly blended. Bring to simmering point; then cook gently for 3–4 minutes, adding salt and black pepper to taste. Put aside while you shell the eggs. Cut them in half and slide into the sauce. Bring back to simmering point over the heat; if the eggs are still warm, 2 minutes will be enough. If they are cold, allow 5 minutes standing at the back of the stove to warm them through. Then stir in the green parts of the scallions; if using them, and pour into the serving dish. Serve with boiled rice; enough for 4 as a main dish, with a green salad on separate plates.

Egg Salad

A little vinegar in the cooking water will aid the shelling of hard-cooked eggs

Serves 2–4

4 large eggs

Salt and freshly ground black pepper to taste

2 tablespoons mayonnaise

2 tablespoons plain yogurt

8 scallions

2–4 lettuce leaves

Optional:

4 slices rye bread, or thin whole wheat bread

A little butter

Hard-cook the eggs. (Put them in a small pan of salted water, bring to the boil, lower the heat, and simmer for 12 minutes. Then plunge them into cold water for 10 minutes, and shell.) Chop them coarsely and put in a bowl. Sprinkle generously with salt and coarsely ground black pepper. Mix the mayonnaise with the yogurt until smooth. Then fold mixture into the eggs, trying not to crush them. Slice the scallions, using the young green leaves as well as the white parts. Mix most of them into the eggs, keeping back a few to scatter over the top. Divide into 2 or 4 helpings and place each helping on a lettuce leaf. Do not chill; serve at room temperature. Enough for 2 as an appetizer or light main dish, or 4 with other dishes. This egg salad also makes good open sandwiches for 4: butter 4 slices rye bread, or thin slices whole wheat bread, lay a lettuce leaf on each, and pile the egg salad on top, scattering the extra chopped scallions over the top.

The hedgehogs dropped their spoons, rose to their feet, and ducked their heads respectfully.

Cauliflower Gratin

Serves 3–4

4 ounces (120 g) raw
long-grained rice
1 medium cauliflower
4 tablespoons (60 g) butter
3 tablespoons (30 g) coarse
fresh bread crumbs

1¼ cups (300 ml) chicken stock
⅔ cup (160 ml) light cream
3 tablespoons flour
Salt and freshly ground black
pepper to taste
4 ounces (120 g) ham, chopped

Cauliflower can
quickly become
overcooked and
ruined

Cook the rice by shaking it into a large pan of lightly
salted boiling water. Bring back to a boil and cook steadily
until a grain is soft when held between the teeth. This will
take 10–12 minutes. Drain in a colander or large strainer
and leave to dry out. Wash the whole cauliflower, put in a
saucepan, and add enough water to barely cover it. Remove
the cauliflower, add a little salt, and bring the water to a
boil over medium heat. Gently drop the cauliflower, stalk
side down, into the boiling water, being careful not to
splash yourself. Bring back to a boil and cook steadily, half
covered by a lid, for about 9 minutes. Test by sticking a
thin skewer or sharp fork into the center of the stalk. As
soon as it is soft, lift cauliflower out and drain. Heat 1
tablespoon of the butter in a frying pan or skillet, over
medium heat; when it is hot, but before it turns brown,
add the bread crumbs and fry until they are a pale golden
brown all over, turning them over and over with a spatula.
Tip onto paper towels to drain. Preheat the oven to 350° F
(175° C). Heat the stock and cream together in a pan,
removing them from the heat before they start to boil; put
aside. Melt the remaining 3 tablespoons butter in a clean
pan and stir in the flour. Cook for 1 minute, stirring, then
gradually pour on the heated stock and cream, stirring until
each newly added batch is smoothly blended into the sauce.
Finally, cook the sauce gently for 3 minutes, stirring often,
and adding salt and pepper to taste. Butter a shallow
ovenproof dish and spread the rice evenly over the bottom.
Divide the cauliflower into fat sprigs and lay on top of the

rice, scattering the chopped ham over and among them. Pour the sauce over the cauliflower so that it is completely covered, and scatter the golden crumbs over the top. Reheat for 15 minutes in the preheated oven. Serves 3–4 as a main dish.

Toad-in-a-Bad-Hole

Serves 4

1¼ cups (175 g) all-purpose flour	A pinch of salt
1 egg plus 1 egg yolk	8 large pork dinner sausages, at room temperature
1 cup (250 ml) milk	

Batter should always be put into an oven which has been fully heated in advance

Preheat the oven to 400° F (205° C). Sift the flour into a large bowl. Make a well in the center and break in the egg and the egg yolk. Have the milk ready in a measuring cup, and as you start to beat the egg with a wire whisk, gradually pour in the milk, a little at a time, with the other hand. Beat the eggs in the center of the bowl, slowly incorporating the flour from around the edges, and pouring the milk into the middle. When all the milk is used up, and the flour mixed in, add a pinch of salt and continue to beat for a couple of minutes until you have a smooth batter. (If you use a food processor, simply put the flour and eggs into the container and process, pouring the milk in slowly through the hole in the lid.) Butter a shallow ovenproof dish and pour a very thin layer of batter into it, just enough to cover the bottom. Put it in the hot oven for 5 minutes. Then take it out and lay the sausages side by side on top of the batter, leaving space between them. Pour the remaining batter over them—it doesn't matter if they aren't quite covered—and return to the oven. Bake for 30 minutes; then turn down the oven to 300° F (150° C) and bake for a further 30 minutes.

"Now cheer up, Toad . . . do try and eat a bit of dinner."

11

Wayfarers' Easy Pizza

Serves 4

Filling:

1 medium onion
2 tablespoons (30 g) butter
2 tablespoons olive oil
1½ cups (350 g) canned
  tomatoes
1 clove garlic
Salt and freshly ground black
  pepper to taste
A pinch of sugar
½ teaspoon dried oregano
  (optional)

Crust:

3 cups (350 g) self-rising flour
A pinch of salt
4 tablespoons (60 g) butter
1 egg
About ½ cup (120 ml) milk

Optional extras:

4 slices bacon, chopped

or

½ (8-ounce/225 g) package
  mozzarella cheese, thinly
  sliced or coarsely grated

or

1 sweet red or green pepper,
  seeded and chopped

or

1 hot chili pepper, seeded
  and finely chopped

or

A few slices pepperoni sausage

Do remember to
stick to either standard
U.S. *or* metric
measurements. The
equivalent weights or
volume measurements
are not exact and have
been rounded off to
make the recipes
easier to follow

This is not a true pizza, which is made with bread dough, but an easy alternative. Preheat the oven to 400° F (205° C). Then make the tomato sauce. Chop the onion and cook gently in the butter and oil in a heavy pan over medium heat, until it becomes translucent. (If using bacon or red or green or chili peppers, they should be added to the onion halfway through its cooking.) Then add the canned tomatoes, coarsely chopped, with their juice, and the garlic, crushed or chopped. Add salt and pepper to taste, a pinch of sugar, and some dried oregano if you have it. Simmer gently, uncovered, stirring occasionally, until nice and thick; this will probably take about 25 minutes. Then leave to cool.

Next make the pizza base. Sift the flour with the salt into a bowl. Cut the butter into small bits and rub into the flour, using your fingertips—do it very lightly. When the mixture looks like bread crumbs, beat the egg with ½ cup milk and stir into the mixture. By now it should all cling together nicely; if not, add a drop or two more milk. Turn out on a floured surface and knead together once or twice; then roll out to make a circle about 10 inches (25 cm) across, or to fit your pan. A proper pizza pan is round, about 10 to 12 inches (25–30 cm) across, with a shallow rim, but a large flan ring can be used instead, or even a flat cookie sheet. It must be well oiled or greased with butter before using.

When the pizza base is in the pan, spoon the sauce over it, leaving a rim about 1 inch (2.5 cm) uncovered around the edge. If you are adding mozzarella cheese or sliced sausage, it should be scattered over the top just before putting in the oven. Bake on the top shelf of the oven for 10 minutes; the edges should be golden brown and puffy. Unlike a real pizza, this can be kept hot for a little while without becoming soggy. Cut in wedges to serve.

Another time, try using the sauce—alone, or with additions of bacon or red or green pepper—as a sauce for spaghetti or noodles.

"Southwards we sailed again at last," continued the Sea Rat, "coasting down the Italian shore, till finally we made Palermo."

Macaroni Cheese

Serves 4

8 ounces (225 g) macaroni
¼ pound (120 g) bacon
5 tablespoons (75 g) butter,
 plus butter to grease dish
3 tablespoons all-purpose
 flour
1 pint (475 ml) milk

⅓ cup (80 ml) light cream
1 cup (120 g) grated
 Cheddar cheese
Salt and freshly ground black
 pepper to taste
½ pound (225 g) tomatoes

Can be made in advance and reheated for 40 minutes at 350° F (175° C)

Bring a large pan of lightly salted water to a boil over medium heat. Then shake in the macaroni gradually, trying to keep the water boiling. Stir once, and cook for 8 minutes (if using quick-cooking macaroni), or according to the directions on the package. Test a piece to see when it is just soft without being mushy, then drain in a colander or large strainer over the sink. Cut the rinds off the bacon and chop the bacon strips. Fry them gently in a frying pan or skillet over medium heat, until crisp, then drain on paper towels. Preheat the oven to 400° F (205° C). Melt 4 tablespoons of the butter, stir in the flour, and cook for 1 minute, stirring all the time. Heat the milk and pour on gradually, stirring constantly until it is blended. Add the cream and most of the grated cheese, reserving about 2 tablespoons, and stir until smooth. Add salt and pepper to taste; then stir in the drained macaroni and the chopped bacon. Mix well, and pour half into a buttered ovenproof dish. Skin the tomatoes by pouring boiling water over them; leave for 1 minute, then plunge into cold water. Pierce the skins, which should then peel off easily; cut the tomatoes in slices and fry them for just 1 minute on each side in the remaining 1 tablespoon butter in a frying pan or skillet over medium heat. Lay them over the macaroni mixture in its dish, and cover with the remaining macaroni mixture. Scatter the 2 tablespoons grated cheese over the top and bake for 20 minutes. Serves 4 as a main dish, with a green salad.

Fish Pie

To prevent an egg taken straight from the refrigerator from breaking in boiling water, pierce it first with a needle

Serves 4

1½ pounds (675 g) potatoes (about 4–5 medium)

¾ cup (180 ml) milk

4 tablespoons (60 g) butter

Salt and freshly ground black pepper to taste

2 tablespoons chopped fresh parsley

4 eggs

1½ pounds (675 g) haddock (or cod) fillet

Boil the potatoes, drain them, and push through a vegetable mill into a clean pan. Dry out by stirring for a few moments over low heat. Heat the milk with the butter and plenty of salt and black pepper in a small pan. When the butter has melted, stir the hot milk into the potatoes, beating well over gentle heat. Stir in the chopped parsley and remove from the heat. Keep hot while you cook the eggs and fish. Bring some lightly salted water to a boil in a smallish saucepan over medium heat, put in the eggs, and cook for exactly 5 minutes; then plunge them into cold water. Put the fish in a broad pan—a sauté pan with a lid is ideal—and barely cover with cold water. Remove the fish, add a little salt to the water, and bring it to a boil. Replace the fish, bring back to the boiling point, then lower the heat until the water just simmers gently. Cover the pan and cook gently for about 8 minutes, until the fish flakes easily with a fork. While it is cooking, shell the eggs carefully and put them in a bowl of hot water to keep warm. To serve, flake the fish, removing all the skin and any bones, and put in the bottom of a greased soufflé dish, which it should half fill. Cover with the potato puree, and lay the soft-cooked eggs on top. Serve as soon as possible. With a salad, this makes a light main dish for 4.

It was a simple but sustaining meal—bacon and broad beans and a macaroni pudding; and, when they had quite done, the Badger settled himself into an arm-chair . . .

Kedgeree

Serves 4

1 cup (225 g) long-grain rice, preferably Uncle Ben's Converted (parboiled)

1 pound (450 g) smoked haddock or cod fillet, or frozen salmon

4 eggs

¼ pound (125 g) butter

Salt and freshly ground black pepper to taste

⅓ cup (80 ml) heavy cream (optional)

When you are making fish dishes it is important to ensure that all the fish bones have been removed

Bring a large pan of lightly salted water to the boil over medium heat; then shake in the rice gradually, trying to keep it on the boil. Stir once, and regulate the heat so that the rice boils steadily without overflowing. Cook for about 16 minutes; then test a grain by squeezing between the fingers, or biting. It should be firm in the center, but not hard. When it is done, pour the contents of the pan through a colander or large strainer over the sink, so that all the water drains away. Rinse under the hot tap, and drain again. Cut the smoked fish fillets into 2 or 3 pieces so that they will fit into a broad shallow pan with a lid. (A sauté pan—like a slightly deeper than usual frying pan with sloping sides—is ideal.) Lay them in it, and add enough cold water to barely cover them. Do not add salt. Bring to the boil, simmer for 4 minutes; then turn off the heat, cover the pan, and leave for 10 minutes. Lift out the fish and allow to cool slightly so that it is possible to handle it without burning your fingers. Break it into large flakes, discarding the skin and any bones. Hard-cook the eggs: put them in a pan, cover with cold water, add salt, and bring to the boil. Cook gently for 12 minutes, then take out the eggs and plunge them into cold water for a minute or two. Remove the shells, cut the eggs in quarters, then cut each quarter across in half, to make squarish chunks. Set a large earthenware or heatproof glass bowl, which has first been greased with butter on the inside, over a saucepan of boiling water. Put a layer of drained rice in the bottom of the bowl, dot with small bits of butter, and sprinkle lightly with salt and freshly ground black pepper. Make a layer of flaked fish over the rice, then a layer of

The Rat, meanwhile, was busy examining the label on one of the beer-bottles. "I perceive this to be Old Burton," he remarked approvingly.

16

pieces of hard-cooked egg, adding salt and pepper over each layer. Continue to make layers of rice, fish, and egg, dotting the rice with butter and adding a little salt and plenty of black pepper, until all is used up. Cover the bowl with foil and stand over simmering water for 20–30 minutes, stirring carefully from time to time. A little heavy cream can be added with the butter if you want a richer version, but this is not essential.

For a special occasion, substitute salmon for the smoked fish, poaching it gently in lightly salted water until it flakes away from the bone easily with a fork—salmon steaks will take 8–10 minutes, depending on the thickness. Kedgeree can be kept warm over hot, but not boiling, water. Alternatively, it can be made in advance, assembled in the earthenware bowl, and only reheated over boiling water 45 minutes before you want to eat. It can even be made a day in advance and kept overnight in the refrigerator.

Herrings in Oatmeal

Preheat the broiler before starting to cook the herrings

Serves 4
8 herrings
A little milk
Medium-ground oatmeal

About 4 tablespoons (60 g) butter
Lemon quarters (optional)

Ask the fish store to fillet the herrings for you—that is to say, to cut off the heads and tails, split them open, and remove the bones. When you get them home, wash them well, discard the roes (or keep them for another dish), and pick out any odd bones that you can find. Put 2 soup plates side by side, one with milk and the other with oatmeal. Pat the fillets dry with paper towels; then dip them first in milk, and then in oatmeal. Heat the broiler. Lay the fillets on the broiler pan, flesh side up, and dot with little bits of butter. Broil gently for about 5 minutes; then turn them over and broil for another 4 minutes. Serve alone, or with lemon quarters. I don't think these need any vegetables, so I allow 2 fish per person. They can be fried in butter if you prefer, but I like them better broiled.

Smoked Haddock (or Cod) with Tomatoes

Serves 4

¾ pound (350 g) tomatoes

3 tablespoons (45 g) butter

1¾ pounds (800 g) smoked haddock (or cod) fillet

1¼ cups (300 ml) half-and-half, or milk and light cream
    mixed

Freshly ground black pepper to taste

1 cup (225 g) rice, boiled

¼ cup (60 g) of rice is an average serving

Preheat the oven to 350° F (175° C). Peel the tomatoes. This is done by putting them in a bowl and pouring boiling water over them. Let them stand for 1 minute; then pour off the hot water and cover them with cold water. When they have cooled, prick the skin with the point of a knife and it will pull off easily. Chop the tomatoes very coarsely. Heat the butter slowly in a frying pan or skillet over low heat. When it has melted, add the tomatoes and cook them gently for 4 minutes. Cut the fish in pieces to fit your dish, choosing a shallow ovenproof one, preferably rectangular in shape. Lay them in the greased dish and pour the tomatoes and their juices over. Add the half-and-half, or milk and cream mixed, then sprinkle with coarsely ground black pepper. Do not add salt. Bake for 25 minutes. Serve with boiled rice and a green salad.

Badger hates Society, and invitations, and dinner, and all that sort of thing.

Leek Pudding

Serves 4—6

Butter to grease bowl
3 cups (350 g) self-rising flour
Salt and freshly ground pepper

6 ounces (175 g) shredded
    suet
6 medium leeks

Remember to watch the water level in the saucepan when boiling or steaming puddings

Find a small pudding basin or mixing bowl—one holding 4 cups (950 ml) will be big enough—and a saucepan large enough to hold it easily. Lay a small cake pan, flan ring, or an old saucer upside down in the pan and stand the bowl on it. Add enough cold water to come halfway up the sides of the bowl, then remove the bowl and grease it inside with butter. Put the pan with the water aside. Sift the flour with a pinch of salt into a large bowl. Add the suet and mix with the fingertips. Add just enough cold water to make it all cling together, mixing it with the blade of a knife. Form into a ball, turn out onto a floured surface, and knead lightly, once or twice. Divide in 2 pieces, one twice as big as the other. Roll out the larger piece to form a circle about ½ inch (1.3 cm) thick; then sprinkle all over with flour and fold in half to form a semicircular-shaped bag. Roll out the closed side of the bag gently to form a sort of pouch shape, so that it will fit into the bottom of the bowl. Open it out and lay it in the greased pudding basin. Cut the washed and trimmed leeks into slices about 1 inch (2.5 cm) thick and pile them, together with a little salt and pepper, into the pastry-lined bowl. Roll out the remaining pastry and lay it over the leeks. Dampen the inner edges and press together to seal, then trim with a knife. Cover with a buttered piece of aluminum foil, doming it to allow the pastry to rise, and tying it with string just under the rim of the basin. Lay the basin in the center of a square cloth or a dish towel and tie the 4 corners together, to form a sort of container. Heat the water in the pan until boiling, then lower the pudding gently into the pan, holding it by the knotted cloth. Cover the pan and keep boiling steadily for 2½ hours, checking every half hour to see if it needs more water. (Add boiling water from a kettle, to come halfway up the sides of the bowl; be careful never to let it boil dry.) This is delicious served with a beef stew.

Boiled Ham with Parsley Sauce

Serves 6

1 (2½–3-pound/1.15–1.35 kg) piece of picnic ham or pork shoulder
1 large onion
1 large carrot
1 leek
2 ribs celery
1 bay leaf
3 whole cloves

Parsley and egg sauce:
2 tablespoons (30 g) butter
1½ tablespoons all-purpose flour
2 cups (450 ml) ham stock
Freshly ground black pepper to taste
A pinch of ground mace or nutmeg
⅓ cup (80 ml) light cream
1 hard-cooked egg, chopped
3 tablespoons chopped fresh parsley

Time should be allowed for soaking smoked ham

If using smoked ham, soak it overnight, or for several hours. Alternatively, if you do not have enough time to soak it, put it in a deep pan, cover with cold water, and bring slowly to a boil. Then throw away the water, cover with fresh cold water, and start the cooking. If the ham has been soaked, throw away the water, put in a pan, and cover with fresh cold water. Add the vegetables, cut in large pieces, the bay leaf, and the cloves—no salt. Bring slowly to a boil, removing any scum that rises to the surface. Lower the heat so that it simmers, cover the pan, and cook for 1¾ hours, or until the ham is tender when pierced with a skewer. When it is cooked, lift out the meat and keep warm while you make the sauce. Strain the stock, discarding the vegetables and flavorings. Taste the stock to make sure it is not too salty to use for the sauce. (If it is, dilute it half-and-half with milk.) Measure 2 cups. Melt the butter in a smallish pan over medium heat, add the flour, and cook for 1 minute, stirring. Add the strained and measured stock, stir until blended, and simmer for 3 minutes, stirring. Add pepper to taste—it probably won't need salt—and a pinch of mace or nutmeg. Stir in the cream, the chopped hard-cooked egg, and the parsley. Carve the ham, pour a little of the sauce over it, and pass the rest. This is good served with boiled or mashed potatoes and boiled carrots.

Potato Cake

Serves 4

Leftover cooked potatoes can also be used for this dish; adjust the quantity of onions and butter accordingly

1½ pounds (675 g) potatoes (about 4–5 medium)

2 large onions

4 tablespoons (60 g) butter

Salt and freshly ground black pepper to taste

Peel the potatoes and put them in a saucepan. Cover with cold water, add a little salt, and bring to a boil over medium heat. Cook steadily until they are just soft when pierced with a skewer; then drain them very well. Push through a food mill into a large bowl or mash with a fork. Cut the onions in half; then slice each half thinly to make semicircular rings. Cook them gently in about two thirds of the butter in a frying pan or skillet. When they are soft and well browned, stir them—and their juices—into the riced potato. Mix well, adding lots of salt and black pepper. Melt the remaining butter in a broad, heavy frying pan or skillet so that the whole surface is greased. Spread the potato mixture evenly over it, right up to the edges, smoothing it evenly with a spatula. Cook over low heat, turning the pan around from time to time, for about 25 minutes. To turn the cake out, lay a flat plate upside down over the pan; then turn both over together, so that the potato cake falls out onto the plate right side up. This is a little tricky to do, so you may find it easier simply to cut the cake into wedges and serve it out of the pan, turning the pieces upside down as you do so. This makes a good supper dish, with fried eggs, bacon, broiled tomatoes, or ham.

Badger summoned them to the table, where he has been busy laying a repast. . . . Conversation was impossible for a long time; and when it was slowly resumed, it was that regrettable sort of conversation that results from talking with your mouth full. The Badger did not mind that sort of thing at all, nor did he take any notice of elbows on the table, or everybody speaking at once.

Bubble and Squeak

Serves 4–5
1½ cups (350 g) mashed potatoes
1½ cups (350 g) chopped cooked cabbage
4 tablespoons (60 g) butter
Salt and freshly ground black pepper to taste

It is always wise to wear an apron when cooking

Mix the mashed potatoes and the chopped cabbage in a
bowl. Melt half the butter in a small saucepan over low
heat and stir into the mixture. Season with plenty of salt
and black pepper. Melt the remaining butter in a frying
pan or skillet; when it is hot, pile in the potato and
cabbage mixture and spread evenly, flattening with a
spatula. Cook over low heat for about 25 minutes, until
nicely browned underneath. Turn out onto a flat dish to
serve. This is very good with cold meat and a tossed green
salad.

Easy Banana Pudding

Serves 4
6 ripe bananas
4 tablespoons (60 ml) syrup
Juice of 2 oranges
Juice of 1 lemon
Cream

To extract the maximum amount of juice from citrus fruit, put the fruit in very hot water and roll it on the table before squeezing

Peel the bananas and cut them in slices. Lay them in a
serving dish. Warm the syrup in a small pan until thinned;
then remove from the heat and stir the fruit juices in. Mix
well, and pour over the bananas. Leave to cool completely;
then chill in the refrigerator for a few hours before serving,
or overnight. Serve with cream. Enough for 4.

Mixed Fruit Fool

Don't try to make this recipe unless you have a blender or food processor

Serves 6

1 cup (225 g) cold cooked rhubarb	1 large banana, or 2 small ones
1 cup (225 g) fresh strawberries, washed and hulled	⅔ cup (160 ml) heavy cream
	⅔ cup (160 ml) plain yogurt
	2 tablespoons superfine sugar

Put the rhubarb, strawberries, and peeled banana, cut into chunks, into the food processor or blender. Add the cream, yogurt, and sugar and process until smoothly blended. Pour into a glass bowl, or individual glasses, and chill for 1 hour before serving. This is especially good served with Refrigerator Cookies (see page 56).

DON'T try to make this unless you have (and are allowed to use) a food processor or blender.

Alternative Version

Serves 6

(Use when strawberries or rhubarb are not available)

1½ cups (350 g) cold cooked rhubarb *or* fresh strawberries, washed and hulled
2 large bananas
⅔ cup (160 ml) heavy cream
⅔ cup (160 ml) plain yogurt
2 tablespoons superfine sugar

Make as above, omitting either strawberries or rhubarb.

It was bubble and squeak between two plates, and its fragrance filled the narrow cell. The penetrating smell of cabbage reached the nose of Toad as he lay prostrate in his misery . . .

Pancakes

Serves 4

Pancake mixture:

¾ cup (80 g) all-purpose flour

A pinch of salt

1 egg

⅔ cup (160 ml) milk, or milk and water mixed

A little butter

Accompaniments:

Superfine sugar and 2 lemons

or 1 (8-ounce/227 g) package cream cheese and 2½
    tablespoons honey

or some cold stewed apples

Pancakes should be cooked in a minimum of fat

If possible, make the pancake mixture 1 hour before using.
If making by hand, sift the flour into a large bowl with the
salt, make a well in the center, and break the egg into it.
Have the milk, or milk and water, in a measuring cup in
your left hand and a wire whisk in your right one
(assuming you are right-handed). Start to beat the egg,
drawing in a little of the flour around the edges, at the
same time pouring in the liquid slowly. Beat constantly,
and try to time it so that by the time all the liquid is used
up, all the flour has been drawn into the batter. Beat for an
extra minute or two, then let stand for an hour if possible.
Beat again just before using. If making in a food processor,
simply put the sifted flour and salt into the container, add
the egg, and process, adding the liquid through the hole in
the lid while processing. Let stand, then process again just
before using.

To make the pancakes: place a small heavy frying pan or
skillet over low heat. When it is hot, rub it with a small
piece of fat—a piece of suet on the end of a fork is best for
this job, but a buttery piece of paper will do. Have a large
spoon or ladle half-full of batter and pour it in, tilting the

pan as you do so, so that it spreads into a nice round shape. Cook gently for about 2 minutes, shaking the pan from time to time. When the pancake slides around easily, it can be turned over carefully, and cooked for another minute, or a minute and a half. The first couple of pancakes are often failures, so don't be ashamed to throw them away. They will get better as you go on and the pan gets hotter. Pile them up on a plate and serve as soon as possible. They can be sprinkled with superfine sugar and served with a lemon quarter or rolled up around a mixture of cream cheese beaten until smooth with a little clear honey, or around some cold stewed apples.

Suddenly the Rat cried, "Hooray!" and then "Hooray-oo-ray-oo-ray-oo-ray!" and fell to executing a feeble jig in the snow.

Jam Roly-Poly (or Roly-Poly Pudding)

2 cups (225 g) self-rising flour
4 ounces (100 g) shredded suet
A pinch of salt
Ice water
½ cup (175 g) raspberry jam

Jam sauce:
½ cup (175 g) raspberry jam
½ cup (175 g) red currant jelly
1 tablespoon brandy

Sift the flour into a large bowl and mix in the shredded suet, rubbing lightly with the fingertips. Add just enough ice water to make it all cling together, mixing with the blade of a knife. Turn out on a floured surface, and knead once, lightly, to form a ball. Roll out to make a strip about 8 inches (20 cm) broad. (Unlike most pastry, suet pastry must be used right away.) Warm the jam slightly, and spread over the dough, leaving about 1½ inches (4 cm) clear around the edges. Dampen the edges and roll up, pressing the edges together to seal and prevent the jam from escaping. Lay on a buttered piece of aluminum foil and roll up loosely, making tucks and pleats here and there to allow the pudding to swell. Lay the whole thing on a cloth and roll up, again loosely, tying the ends with string, and leaving long ends if planning to boil it. If you have a steamer large enough—a combined steamer/asparagus pan, or a wok with steaming tray and lid—bring some water to a boil and lower in the pudding on its perforated tray. If you don't have a steamer, the pudding can be boiled; bring some water to a boil in a kettle or oval casserole and lower in the pudding by the string. In either case, allow 1½ hours cooking, checking often to make sure the water is not evaporating, and that it is boiling steadily.

Alternatively, the pudding may be baked, which means that it does not have to be wrapped in foil and cloth. Simply lay on a greased baking sheet and bake for 40 minutes in an oven preheated to 350° F (175° C). Ten minutes before it is ready, make the sauce. Warm the jam and jelly together in a small pan, adding the brandy. Mix well, and serve in a heated sauceboat.

Apple Snow

Serves 4
2 pounds (900 g) cooking apples
¼ cup (60 g) sugar
2 egg whites
Cream

For successfully beaten egg whites, the whisk and bowl must be completely free from grease and water, and the egg whites completely free of yolk

Peel and core the apples and cut in slices. Put them in a saucepan with 2 tablespoons water and the sugar. Cook gently until soft; then push through a medium food mill, or a coarse sieve, or put briefly in a food processor. Pour into a bowl and leave to cool. When they are cold, beat the egg whites until stiff and fold into the apple puree. Tip into a bowl and chill in the refrigerator for an hour or two. Serve with cream.

. . . looking back, they saw the whole mass of the Wild Wood, dense, menacing, compact, grimly set in vast white surroundings; simultaneously they turned and made swiftly for home, for firelight and the familiar things it played on, for the voice, sounding cheerily outside their window, of the river that they knew and trusted in all its moods . . .

2
Food for Staying in Bed

Here are a few things to make, either for someone who is ill in bed, or for yourself when you are not feeling really well. Anyone who is ill, especially with a fever, should drink a lot of fluids, so things like lemonade are always useful. People with colds or sore throats will like the Honey and Lemon Drink, while eggnog is good for feeding someone when they are not feeling hungry. Another useful drink is Milk Shake Ripple. Even when people aren't hungry, they may be tempted by Moly's Marmite Soldiers, or marmalade sandwiches. The latter can be made with either white or whole wheat buttered bread and a good marmalade; it is important that they should be very small and delicate, with the crusts cut off. For an evening meal, both Chicken Noodle Soup and Potato Soup are good, while a plain boiled egg, or a poached egg on buttered toast, will appeal to most invalids.

Chicken Noodle Soup

Serves 3–4

4 cups (950 ml) chicken stock (homemade or made with
    bouillon cubes)
3 small carrots, peeled or scraped and thickly sliced
3 small leeks, well washed and thickly sliced
4 ounces (120 g) green beans (about ½ cup cut in chunks)
3 small tomatoes
2 tablespoons (30 g) vermicelli
Salt and freshly ground black pepper to taste
2–4 tablespoons chopped cooked chicken (optional)

Home-made chicken stock (optional)
1 chicken carcass
1 onion, halved
1 carrot, cut in pieces
1 rib celery, cut in pieces
1 bay leaf
Salt and freshly ground pepper to taste

If you have the remains of a cold roast chicken, this will be
delicious; cut off all the scraps of flesh and reserve. For
homemade chicken stock put the carcass in a pot with
some flavoring vegetables—onion, carrot, celery—and bay
leaf; add salt and pepper and cover with cold water, about
6 cups (1.5 l). Bring slowly to the boil, cover the pot, and
simmer for 3 hours. Strain the stock and leave to cool, then
put overnight in the refrigerator. Next day remove the fat
from the surface and measure the stock. You should have
about 4 cups, but the quantities are not important.
Alternatively, you can make the stock from bouillon cubes,
dissolving them with double the amount of water
recommended in the directions on the package. (The stock
will become stronger and saltier during the cooking.)
Whichever base you are using, pour it into a saucepan.

Homemade
chicken stock
should be made a
day in advance

In another pan, bring 3¼ cups (750 ml) lightly salted cold water to the boil, and add the sliced carrots. Cook for 5 minutes; then add the sliced leeks and the chunked string beans. After another 10 minutes add the tomatoes, which you have skinned (see recipe for Smoked Haddock [or Cod] with Tomatoes, page 18, for instructions), and cut in quarters. Cook for another 6–8 minutes, then test the vegetables to see if they are tender. As soon as they are soft, turn off the heat. Reheat the chicken stock. Lift the cooked vegetables out of the pan with a slotted spoon and put them in the chicken stock. Reheat the vegetable cooking water until it boils and add the vermicelli. Cook for 5 minutes; then pour through a strainer and add the vermicelli to the chicken soup. Add salt and pepper to taste, also any remains of chicken (if you have them), neatly chopped and free from skin and bone. Let the soup stand for 5 minutes before serving. If for an invalid, serve in a small cup with a dry cracker. Leave the rest of the soup to cool, then stand it in the refrigerator. If for an ordinary meal, this will serve 3–4, with crusty French bread, and a tossed green salad to follow. It is a meal in itself, especially if it has pieces of chopped chicken in it.

Supper was a most cheerful meal; but very shortly afterwards a terribly sleepy Mole had to be escorted upstairs by his considerate host.

Potato Soup

Serves 4
1 large onion
4 tablespoons (60 g) butter
2 large potatoes
2 cups (475 ml) chicken stock
Salt and freshly ground black pepper to taste
2 cups (475 ml) milk or half-and-half
2 tablespoons chopped fresh parsley

Chop the onion and cook it very slowly in the butter in a heavy saucepan, stirring now and then. When it becomes soft and almost transparent, add the potatoes, which you have peeled and sliced. (After peeling, cut each potato in half lengthwise, then lay them cut side down and slice thinly downward.) Cook the potatoes and onions together for a moment or two, until well mixed and coated with butter. Then heat the stock; if you have no homemade chicken stock, use a bouillon cube diluted with twice as much water as instructed on the package. Add the stock to the sliced vegetables and bring to a boil, adding salt and pepper to taste. Simmer gently for about 25 minutes, until the potatoes are soft when pierced with a fork. Heat the milk or half-and-half, stopping before it boils, and add to the soup. Stir well, adding more salt and pepper as needed. This soup can be pushed through a coarse food mill, pureed briefly in a food processor or blender, or left as it is. Stir in the parsley just before serving. This is a good soup to make for someone who has been ill, as it is very simple and easy to digest.

Onions that are being cooked in butter in a saucepan or frying pan should be set over low heat; otherwise they will brown and burn. Covering with a lid will help them to sweat and soften

Very hot buttered toast, cut thick, very brown on both sides, with the butter running through the holes in it in great golden drops, like honey from the honeycomb.

32

Moly's Marmite Soldiers

Do remember that kitchen knives can be very sharp

Thick slices white bread
Butter
Marmite (concentrated yeast extract)

Toast the bread and cut off the crusts. While still hot, spread with butter and dab with Marmite. Cut into fingers and serve at once. This is one of those curious foods that people sometimes feel like, even when they are not well enough to be hungry.

"Dear, kind Rat," murmured Toad, "how little you realize my condition, and how very far I am from 'jumping up' now—if ever! But do not trouble about me. I hate being a burden to my friends, and I do not expect to be one much longer. Indeed, I almost hope not."

A Simple Rice Pudding

Serves 4
¼ cup (60 g) long-grain rice
2 tablespoons (30 g) sugar
2½ cups (600 ml) milk
2 tablespoons (30 g) butter

Before starting, a suitable dish should be found and prepared

Preheat the oven to 250° F (125° C). Put the rice in a strainer and wash by running cold water through it. Drain well. Using a buttery piece of paper, grease an earthenware or Pyrex pie dish. Put the rice in the bottom and add the sugar. Pour the milk over them and stir once or twice with a fork, breaking up any lumps in the rice. Cut the butter in small bits and dot over the top. Bake for 2 hours in the oven. By the end of the cooking time, the top should be a golden brown and most of the milk should have been absorbed by the rice. This is good either hot or cold, or just warm. For a treat, serve warm, with very cold stewed apples and a pitcher of cream.

. . . a dark hole in the bank opposite, just above the water's edge, caught his eye, and dreamily he fell to considering what a nice snug dwelling-place it would make for an animal with few wants and fond of a bijou riverside residence . . .

Sliced Bananas in Orange Gelatin

Start well ahead to allow time for the gelatin to set, either in the morning for the evening meal, or a day ahead for lunchtime

Serves 4–6
10 medium oranges
½ cup (120 g) sugar
1 lemon
1 (½-ounce/15 g) envelope gelatin
2 ripe bananas

Pare the rind of 1 orange and put it in a bowl; this is easily done with a sharp potato peeler. Put the sugar in a small pan with ⅔ cup (160 ml) water and bring to the boil. Boil for 2 minutes, until the sugar has melted, then pour—while still boiling—over the orange rind. Leave for 10 minutes to infuse while you squeeze the juice of all the fruit. Pour it into a measuring cup through a strainer, adding the orange syrup. You should have just under 2½ cups (600 ml). Calculate how much water it needs to make up to 2½ cups and put this in a small jug or a measuring cup. Shake in the gelatin and stand the jug in a pan with hot water to come halfway up it. Heat until almost boiling; when the gelatin has melted, pour it onto the orange liquid and strain once more. Leave to cool completely. Peel the bananas and slice quite thickly and lay them in a dish, or divide them between several small dishes, one for each person. Pour the orange gelatin over them and chill in the refrigerator until set; this may take 2 hours, so allow plenty of time. Serve alone, or with cream. If you prefer, tangerine or tangelo or clementine sections may be used instead of sliced bananas; in this case substitute 2 peeled tangerines, tangelos, or clementines for the bananas, after dividing up into sections.

Milk Shake Ripple

Serves 1–2
1 egg
¼ cup (60 g) berries, fresh or frozen: strawberries,
    raspberries, blueberries, or whatever you prefer
1 banana
2 tablespoons frozen orange juice concentrate
1 tablespoon honey (optional)
⅓ cup (80 ml) milk

Put all the ingredients in a blender or food processor and
whiz until blended. Pour into glasses and either serve
immediately, or put in the freezer for 15–30 minutes, until
semifrozen, when it will be almost thick enough to eat with
a spoon. This milk shake is very nourishing and can take
the place of a meal. For invalids, do not freeze.

Don't try to make this recipe unless you have a food processor or blender

Eggnog

Serves 1
1 egg yolk
½ tablespoon superfine sugar
½ tablespoon brandy or whisky
1¼ cups (300 ml) milk

If using a food processor, put the egg yolk with the sugar
in the container. Process until blended; then add the brandy
(or whisky) and process again. Heat the milk in a small
pan until it reaches the boiling point, then pour the boiling
milk through the lid of the food processor while processing.
(If using a blender, add the milk a little at a time,
blending—with the lid on—after each addition.) Pour
through a strainer into a glass. Serve immediately. If you
have an electric hand beater, use this to beat the egg and
sugar. If making by hand, with no electric equipment
whatever, you must beat very thoroughly with a wire whisk.

Pour the eggnog into a glass through a fine strainer in order to catch any little strands of egg

They got the boat out, and the Rat took the sculls, paddling with caution. Out in midstream there was a clear, narrow track that faintly reflected the sky; but wherever shadows fell on the water from bank, bush, or tree, they were as solid to all appearance as the banks themselves, and the Mole had to steer with judgment accordingly.

Honey and Lemon Drink

Serves 1
1 lemon
1–2 tablespoons honey
2–3 tablespoons whisky (optional)

When pouring hot liquid into a glass, always remember to stand a spoon in the glass first to prevent its cracking

Squeeze the juice of 1 lemon into a glass or mug. Add 1–2 tablespoons honey, depending on your taste. If using a glass, leave the spoon standing in it while you fill it up with very hot water; otherwise the glass may crack. Stir until the honey has melted; drink while hot. This is very good for colds or sore throats, or when you are tired. Adults may prefer this with little a whisky added just before drinking.

"When the last cask was in, we went and refreshed and rested, and sat late into the night, drinking with our friends"

Lemonade

Don't try to make this recipe unless you have a blender or food processor

3 lemons
3 tablespoons sugar (preferably superfine)
5 cups (1.2 l) cold water

Wash the lemons and cut in quarters; then cut each quarter in half to make 8 pieces. Put them in the food processor or blender with the sugar and water. Process briefly, just until the lemons are coarsely chopped, then pour through a strainer into a large jug. Chill in the refrigerator and serve with ice. For a mixed orange-and-lemonade, use 2 oranges, 2 lemons, and 2 tablespoons sugar.

Lemonade II

Always check to see that you have the right equipment before beginning a recipe. In the case of this one, it is essential to use a heatproof and not a plain glass jug

3 lemons
3 tablespoons sugar (preferably superfine)
5 cups (1.2 l) boiling water

Wash the lemons and chop them in smallish pieces, saving any juice that runs out. Put them in a heatproof jug (not glass), with the sugar. Pour on the boiling water and let stand for 20 minutes, then strain into a glass jug. Chill in the refrigerator, and serve with ice.

3
Food for the
Storage Cupboard

Sometimes it's fun to cook, perhaps on a rainy day, even if
you don't actually need anything to eat that day. This is a
good time to make something for the days ahead—not too
far ahead, but for the weekend, or a picnic in the near
future, or a party of some sort. Sometimes there is food
going free, like blackberries in the woods, or shrimp on the
seashore; this is the time to make jelly, or potted shrimp. If
you have a blender or food processor, or a mortar and
pestle, good paste can be made with chicken or fresh or
smoked fish; these can be kept for a few days in the
refrigerator—or longer if properly sealed, or put in the
freezer—and come in handy for picnics, suppers, or cold
meals of any sort.

Ratty's Potted Meat

Serves 4

12 ounces (350 g) cold roast chicken or beef (about 1½
    cups chopped)

or

6 ounces (175 g) cold roast or boiled chicken *and* 6 ounces
    (175 g) cold ham

8 tablespoons (120 g) butter

Salt and freshly ground black pepper to taste

A pinch of cayenne pepper

2 teaspoons lemon juice, if using chicken

Sprig of parsley for garnish

Do remember that
kitchen knives can
be very sharp

Weigh the meat after discarding all skin, bone, fat, and
gristle. (If you do not have enough, don't worry; just weigh
it anyway and reduce the butter accordingly.) Chop it in
very small pieces. If using a food processor, process until
reduced to a paste. The butter must be quite cold; it can be
used straight from the refrigerator. Cut it in very small bits.
Add it to the meat and process again until they are blended
together. Otherwise, put the finely chopped meat in a
mortar and pound; then add the butter by degrees and
continue to pound until all is blended into a smooth paste.
Add salt and pepper to taste—if you are using ham, salt
will not be needed—and a very little cayenne. Add the
lemon juice, if using chicken, and pile into a small china
dish which it fills to the rim; one holding 2 cups (475 ml)
will be perfect. Alternatively, fill 2 or 3 smaller dishes.
Chill in the refrigerator for a few hours before serving.
Garnish with a tiny sprig of parsley and eat with hot toast.
Enough for 4 as an appetizer. This is also good for taking
on picnics; in this case, eat with crusty French bread. It will
keep for 2–3 days in the refrigerator; if you want to keep it
longer, put it in a slightly larger dish and pour a layer of
melted fat—butter or lard—over the top, then chill to set.
It will then keep for 2–3 weeks in the refrigerator.

Potted Fish

Serves 3—4

When you are making fish dishes it is important to ensure that all the bones are removed

6 ounces (175 g) cooked salmon, free from skin and bone

5 tablespoons (75 g) butter

½ teaspoon salt

Freshly ground black pepper to taste

2 teaspoons lemon juice

If using raw salmon, allow 8 ounces (225 g). Lay it on a buttered enamel plate, dot with small bits of butter, pour over 1 tablespoon hot water, and cook, covered with another plate, over a pan of boiling water for 10 minutes. Remove from the pan, uncover, and leave to cool. Discard all skin and bone, chop, and put in a food processor if you are using one. Otherwise, chop finely, then mash with a fork, and finally beat against the sides of a bowl with the back of a wooden spoon, until reduced to a paste. Cut the butter in small pieces and add to the food processor, or beat in by hand with the back of the wooden spoon. Finally, add salt and black pepper and the lemon juice. When all is smooth and blended, pile into a small dish— one holding 1¼ cups (300 ml) will do nicely—and chill in the refrigerator. If you want to keep this longer than 24 hours, seal it by pouring a layer of melted butter all over the top, so that the fish is protected from the air. It can then be kept for up to a week in the refrigerator, or can be frozen. Serve with toast.

"No bread!" groaned the Mole dolorously; "no butter, no . . ." "No pate de foie gras, no champagne," continued the Rat, grinning.

Mole, as he took the head of the table in a sort of dream, saw a lately barren board set thick with savoury comforts; saw his little friends' faces brighten and beam as they fell to without delay; and then let himself loose—for he was famished indeed— on the provender so magically provided, thinking what a happy home-coming this had turned out, after all.

Kipper Paste

It is nearly always
a good idea to take
the butter out of
the refrigerator an
hour before using it

Serves 3–4

1 plump kipper, or ½ package
  frozen kipper fillets
2 ounces (60 g) cream cheese
4 tablespoons (60 g) butter
1 tablespoon lemon juice

Freshly ground black pepper
  to taste
Sprig of fresh parsley
Toasted whole wheat bread
Butter

Put the kipper in a dish and pour boiling water over it;
leave for 10 minutes, then lift out and leave to cool
slightly. If using frozen kipper fillets, cook according to
instructions on the package, and leave to cool. Scrape away
all skin and bone, and weigh or measure the flesh; you
should have 4–5 ounces (120–150 g)—about ½ cup or a
little more. If using a food processor, put the pieces of
kipper in it and process until reduced to a paste. Then add
the cream cheese and butter and process until all is
smoothly blended, adding the lemon juice and freshly
ground black pepper to taste. If you have a mortar and
pestle, this can be used instead of the food processor. Chop
the fish finely, then pound until reduced to a paste. Add
the cheese and pound again, then the butter, and repeat
until you have a fairly smooth paste, adding lemon juice
and black pepper at the end. If you have neither a food
processor nor a mortar and pestle, chop the fish as fine as
possible and beat it in a large bowl, mashing it against the
sides of the bowl with the back of a wooden spoon. It
should be sieved at this stage, before adding the cheese and
butter, but if you don't mind a rough paste you need not
bother. (A food mill with a medium mesh is a quicker
alternative, unless the sieve is quite coarse.) Then beat in
the cheese and butter in small bits and season as usual.
After making, pile the paste into a small dish which it fills
nicely and chill in the refrigerator for 2–3 hours before
serving. This can be kept for 2–3 days before eating, or
eaten the same day. If you want to keep it longer, pour a

layer of melted butter over the top so that it is airtight, then cool and keep for up to 2 weeks in the refrigerator. To serve, put a tiny sprig of parsley in the center, and eat with toasted whole wheat bread and cold butter. This also makes good sandwiches—using whole wheat bread—for taking on a picnic.

Marseilles Potted Shrimp

Serves 2

1 pound (450 g) unshelled shrimp, or 6 ounces (175 g) shelled ones
6–8 tablespoons (90–120 g) butter
¼ bay leaf
Freshly ground black pepper to taste

A pinch of ground mace or nutmeg
Sprig of parsley for garnish
Toasted whole wheat bread
½ lemon, cut in 2 quarters

Time should be allowed to thaw out frozen shrimp before starting

Shell the shrimp; you should have about 6 ounces (¾ cup). Stand a small earthenware bowl over a saucepan of simmering water and melt the butter in this. Add the bay leaf, and after the butter has melted, the shrimp. Mix them gently with the butter, adding some freshly ground black pepper and the mace or nutmeg. Stand over gentle heat for 10 minutes, stirring occasionally. Then discard the bay leaf and spoon the shrimp into a small dish which they almost fill; a straight-sided dish holding about 1 cup (250 ml) will be about right. Pour over enough of the butter to almost cover them, and leave to cool. Once they are cool, put them in the refrigerator to set. These should be eaten within 2 days of making; if you want to keep them longer, pour a second layer of melted butter over the first one after it has set, so that the shrimp are completely covered with an airtight seal. They can then be kept up to 2 weeks in the refrigerator, but are not quite so good as when eaten within 2 days. To serve, put a tiny sprig of parsley in the center of the dish, and eat with toasted whole wheat bread and lemon quarters.

46

Pickled Onions

It is very easy to pour boiling vinegar over yourself instead of into the jars, so take great care when pickling onions

Makes one pound

1 pound (450 g) small white onions

¾ cup (175 g) salt

6¼ cups (1.75 l) water

2½ cups (600 ml) cider vinegar

1 tablespoon soft brown sugar

1 tablespoon pickling spice

Trim the onions, cutting off the tops and bottoms but leaving the skins on. Put them in a deep bowl. Boil the salt and water together, until the salt has dissolved; then remove from the heat and leave to cool. Strain, and pour half over the onions. Leave them for 24 hours; then strain off the water and skin the onions. Put them back in the bowl and cover with the rest of the salty water. Lay a small plate on top of them so that they are kept submerged. Leave for 48 hours; then lift them out with a slotted spoon and pack into broad-mouthed preserving jars, which have first been sterilized. Boil the vinegar with the sugar and spice and, taking great care not to spill it over yourself, pour over the onions in the warm sterilized jars, filling them to the brim. Cover the jars tightly. DO be careful when pouring the boiling vinegar into the jars! Have them standing on a wooden surface that is easy to clean. Wipe the jars clean with a hot wet cloth before sealing.

"Talk of shell-fish! Why, sometimes I dream of the shell-fish of Marseilles, and wake up crying!"

Nutty Spice Island Mixture

Makes about 2 cups (475 ml)
6 tablespoons (90 g) sesame seeds
3 tablespoons (45 g) hazelnuts
2 tablespoons (30 g) ground coriander
2 tablespoons (30 g) ground cumin
½ teaspoon salt
¼ teaspoon freshly ground black pepper

Don't try to
make this recipe
unless you have a
blender or food
processor

Sesame seeds and hazelnuts can be bought in health food stores; coriander and cumin are found in Indian, Pakistani, or Middle Eastern shops, if you cannot find them on your supermarket spice shelves. Cook the sesame seeds in a dry frying pan or skillet, shaking them over very gentle heat, turning them over every now and then with a spatula, so that they color evenly. When they are pale golden, put them aside and do the same thing with the hazelnuts. When these have been lightly toasted, rub off their skins in a dry cloth. Leave to cool. When both the seeds and the nuts have cooled, put them in the blender with the coriander, cumin, salt, and pepper. Process until they are reduced to a finely ground mixture, then pack in a storage jar and cover tightly. Store in a cool dark closet and use as required. This mixture is delicious eaten with hard-cooked eggs and whole wheat bread and butter, for picnics, light meals, or snacks. Can be kept for 2–3 months.

"Well, well," said the Mole, moving towards the supper-table; "supposing you talk while I eat. Not a bite since breakfast! O my! O my!" And he sat down and helped himself liberally to cold beef and pickles.

Tomato Chutney

**The jars should be
sterilized while the
chutney is cooking**

Makes 3 pounds
3 pounds (1.35 kg) tomatoes
½ pound (225 g) apples (1½ medium)
½ pound (225 g) onions
½ cup (120 g) raisins (dark or golden)
1 tablespoon salt
1 teaspoon freshly ground black pepper
1 pound (450 g) (2 cups) soft brown sugar
1 teaspoon mustard seed, or ½ teaspoon mustard powder
1 teaspoon ground allspice
3¾ cups (900 ml) cider vinegar

Skin the tomatoes. (See recipe for Smoked Haddock {or
Cod] with Tomatoes, page 18, for instructions.) Chop
them coarsely and put them in a preserving pan if you have
one, or a broad saucepan with a thick bottom. Peel, core,
and chop the apples; add them to the tomatoes. Chop the
onions and add them also, with the raisins. Scatter the salt,
pepper, brown sugar, mustard seed or powder, and allspice
over them, and pour on the vinegar. Put over a gentle heat
and bring slowly to the boil. Simmer slowly, uncovered,
until the mixture is thick and jammy. This will probably
take about 1½ hours. You must watch it carefully, stirring
every now and then, and skimming off the scum from the
surface. When it is good and thick, spoon it into hot
sterilized jars, taking great care not to burn yourself. (See
page 51.) Wipe off any drips with a hot damp cloth. Leave
to cool, then cover closely and store in a dark cool
cupboard. Keep for 2 weeks before eating. This will fill 3
(1-pound/450 g) jars. Serve with bread and cheese, or cold
meat.

By-ways Blackberry Jelly

Makes about 3 pounds (1.35 kg)
3 pounds (1.35 kg) cooking apples
1 pound (450 g) blackberries
2 pounds (900 g) sugar
Juice of 1 lemon

Stand the jars to be filled on a surface which is easy to clean, as there are bound to be drips

Wash the apples and cut in quarters; do not peel or remove the cores. Put them with the blackberries in a large pan and add enough cold water to come level with the fruit. Bring slowly to a boil over medium heat and keep boiling steadily for 30 minutes, till the apples are soft and pulpy. Pour into a jelly bag (see note below) and leave overnight to drip into a large pan. Next day, throw away the contents of the jelly bag and measure the juice. For every 2½ cups (600 ml) of juice allow 1 pound (450 g) sugar. Put the sugar in a dry pan and warm it gently over low heat for a few moments. Add the juice and the lemon juice. Bring to a boil, skimming off the scum that rises to the surface. When it is clear, allow about 20 minutes steady boiling; then test for setting. Put a teaspoonful of the juice in a saucer and put in the refrigerator ice compartment or freezer for 2–3 minutes. When cold, push the surface gently with a fingertip; if the jelly wrinkles, it is ready to set. Otherwise, continue boiling for another 5–10 minutes, then test again. When setting point is reached, spoon into hot sterilized jars, taking great care not to burn yourself (see note) and leave to cool, after wiping off any drips with a hot damp cloth. When cool, lay a little circle of wax paper or parchment dipped in liquid paraffin or brandy on the top of the jam, then screw down the lids, or cover with more greaseproof paper and a rubber band. Label clearly and store in a cool dark cupboard.

DO improvise if you don't have a jelly bag. Line a colander or large strainer with a large square of doubled cheesecloth and set the colander over a large bowl. If you can find a chair with a cane seat, stand the bowl under the seat, on the floor. Tip the jelly into the cloth-lined colander, then tie the corners of the cheesecloth together with a longish piece of string, so that it forms a bag. Lift this out of the colander and tie the string through the chair seat so that the bag hangs suspended over the bowl. Remove the colander and leave to drip. If you don't have a cane-seated chair, stand one wooden chair on top of another, with its legs sticking in the air. Stand the bowl on the upside-down seat, and tie the bag to the ends of the legs. DON'T try to hurry the dripping by squeezing the bag. This will make the jelly cloudy. It must be left to drip undisturbed.

To sterilize the jam jars beforehand: after washing and drying, stand them upside down on the oven rack, at least 1 inch (2.5 cm) apart. Turn the oven on to the lowest possible heat and leave for 20 minutes, then turn off the oven and leave the jars inside until ready to fill. They must be hot, or warm at least, before filling or they may crack.

He talked of the reddening of apples around, of the browning nuts, of jams and preserves and the distilling of cordials; till by easy stages such as these he reached mid-winter, its hearty joys and its snug home life, and then he became simply lyrical.

Crab Apple Jelly

Makes about 3 pounds (1.35 kg)
4 pounds (1.75 kg) crab apples
About 2 pounds (900 g) sugar
Juice of 1 lemon

An important rule
in cooking is
always to read the
recipe through
before starting

Wash the crab apples and cut them in quarters; do not peel
or remove the cores. Put them in a large pan and add
enough cold water to come level with the fruit. Bring
slowly to the boil and keep boiling steadily for 40 minutes,
until the crab apples are soft and pulpy. Pour into a jelly
bag (see note on page 50), and leave overnight to drip.
Next day, throw away the contents of the jelly bag and
measure the juice. For every 2½ cups (600 ml) of juice,
allow 1 pound (450 g) sugar. Put the sugar in a dry pan
and warm it gently over low heat for a few moments. Add
the juice and the lemon juice. Bring to a boil, skimming off
the scum that rises to the surface with a straining spoon.
When it is clear, and no more scum forms, allow it to boil
undisturbed for about 20 minutes, then test for setting (see
page 50). When setting point is reached, spoon into hot
sterilized jars, taking great care not to burn yourself (see
page 51), and leave to cool, after wiping off any drips or
smears with a hot damp cloth. When cool, lay a small
circle of wax paper or parchment dipped in liquid paraffin
or brandy on the top of the jam, then screw down the lid,
or cover with more greaseproof paper and tie with string.
Label and store in a cool dark cupboard.

They landed, and pushed through the blossom and scented herbage and undergrowth that led up to the level ground, till they stood on a little lawn of a marvellous green, set round with Nature's own orchard-trees— crab-apple, wild cherry, and sloe.

53

Plum Jam

Makes about 3 pounds
4 pounds (1.75 kg) plums
4 pounds (1.75 kg) granulated sugar

The jars should be hot, or at least warm, before being filled

Preheat the oven to 300° F (150° C). Pull the stalks off the plums and put the whole fruit in a pot with a lid. Add 2½ cups (600 ml) water, cover, and cook in the oven for 2 hours. Warm the sugar in a heavy pan over low heat. Add the plums and their juice and bring slowly to the boil. Boil steadily, quite fast, for about 8 minutes, until setting point is reached (see page 50). Skim off the surface scum with a draining spoon, then ladle the jam into hot sterilized jars, taking great care not to burn yourself (see page 51). Wipe off any drips with a hot damp cloth. When the jam has cooled, lay a circle of wax paper or parchment dipped in liquid paraffin or brandy on top to prevent a mold forming, and cover with a lid, or more paper tied with string or a rubber band.

Frozen Milky Way

Cut a Milky Way bar in 4, wrap in plastic wrap, and freeze. It is important to cut it up first, as, once frozen, it is almost impossible to bite through. Alternatively, you can wrap the pieces separately, for small snacks.

Make sure that there is always a ready supply of plastic wrap in the kitchen, as well as aluminum foil and wax paper

Chocolate Chip Cookies

Try to remember to take the butter out of the refrigerator an hour before using it

Makes about 30 cookies
6 tablespoons (75 g) unsalted (sweet) butter
6 tablespoons (75 g) superfine sugar
4 tablespoons (60 g) light brown sugar
1 egg
1½ cups (175 g) self-rising flour
A pinch of salt
4 tablespoons (60 g) chocolate chips

Preheat the oven to 375° F (190° C), and rub 2 cookie sheets with light vegetable oil. Cream the butter, either by hand or in a food processor, sift in the sugar, and cream again. Add the brown sugar, and beat well until blended smoothly. Beat the egg and stir it in alternately with the sifted flour and salt, beating until all is well mixed. Finally, stir in the chocolate chips. Using 2 teaspoons, drop little mounds of the soft dough, about ½ teaspoonful only, onto the cookie sheets, leaving at least 1 inch (2.5 cm) between each one, as they spread while baking. Bake for about 12– 15 minutes, until they are golden brown. Lift them off the sheets while they are still warm, and lay them on a rack to cool. Don't worry if some of them have run together; they will break apart easily as they cool. Keep in the refrigerator, or freeze half.

The Badger's winter stores, which indeed were visible everywhere, took up half the room— piles of apples, turnips, and potatoes, baskets full of nuts, and jars of honey . . .

Refrigerator Cookies

6 tablespoons (90 g) butter
½ cup (120 g) superfine sugar
1 egg
1½ cups (175 g) self-rising flour
A pinch of salt

Have the butter at room temperature—not straight out of
the refrigerator. Cut it in bits, put in a bowl, and cream it
by mashing it against the sides of the bowl with the back
of a wooden spoon. When it is smooth, sift the sugar
(shake through a sieve or strainer), and add to the butter
by degrees, continuing to beat it with the spoon, so that
the butter and sugar are thoroughly blended. (All this can
be quickly done in an electric mixer or food processor.)
Break the egg into a small bowl and beat with a whisk,
then pour it into the creamed butter-sugar mixture, beating
it in with the spoon. Sift the flour with a pinch of salt, and
add to the mixture, stirring it in well. When all is smooth
and well mixed, put the bowl in the refrigerator for 30
minutes, until the mixture is firm enough to handle easily.
Once it has firmed up, form it into a sausage shape by
rolling (with the hands, not a rolling pin) on a flat surface
until you have an even roll about 2 inches (5 cm) thick.
Wrap it in plastic wrap and store in the refrigerator until
needed. To bake, preheat the oven to 350° F (175° C).
Unwrap the cookie dough and cut it in thin slices while
still hard, using a sharp knife. Have an oiled cookie sheet
ready, or two if you plan to bake a lot of cookies. (Either
rub a few drops sunflower or peanut oil over the surface of
the sheet, or use a bit of paper with a small piece of soft
butter to grease the sheet.) Lay the cookie slices on it,
allowing a space between each one, as they spread during
the baking. Bake them for about 6–8 minutes, until they
are a pale golden color, rather like straw. When they are
ready, lift out the cookie sheet and allow the cookies to

cool for a moment or two, then lift them off carefully, using a spatula. They will still be soft, but if you wait until they cool completely on the sheet, they will become brittle and break when you lift them. Lay them on a flat surface to cool completely; they will become hard enough to lift with the fingers and lay on a plate. Bake only as many as you need at any one time; simply rewrap the rest of the roll and return to the refrigerator, where it will keep for weeks. These little cookies are delicious with ice cream, fruit fools, or simply for tea.

"And the Wild Wooders have been living in Toad Hall ever since," continued the Rat; *"and going on simply anyhow! Lying in bed half the day, and breakfast at all hours, and the place in such a mess (I'm told) it's not fit to be seen! Eating your grub, and drinking your drink . . . they're telling the tradespeople and everybody that they've come to stay for good."*

4
Food for Excursions

These are things that can be easily transported, for picnics and outings of all sorts. Some of them are for one person, but they can just as easily be made for two or three. Remember to have plenty of plastic wrap or aluminum foil for wrapping food in; a clean damp dish towel is also good for keeping sandwiches from drying out, or for wrapping lettuce leaves. Cardboard egg cartons are useful for carrying stuffed eggs, which squash easily; they can be cut down for carrying 2 eggs. Good sandwiches can be made with French bread, if you don't mind chewing, or with crackers as well as with sliced white or whole wheat bread. Try unevenly chopped chocolate, spread between 2 slices of white bread buttered with unsalted (sweet) butter, or use wholemeal cookies or plain crackers, water biscuits, or matzos and spread them with cream cheese, Cheddar cheese, or processed cheese. Small pies and pasties are especially good when one is hungry, particularly if they are still warm. If you wrap them in aluminum foil while they are hot they will keep warm for a long time. Don't forget the drink; cans of cola or orange soda can be put in the freezer for an hour or two before leaving to get really cold; don't do this with bottles, as they may burst if left too long.

Riverside Sandwich

Serves 1

2 slices whole wheat bread	2–3 lettuce leaves
Butter	2 scallions
Cream cheese	2–3 sprigs watercress
A dash of Marmite (optional), or a pinch of salt	2–3 sprigs parsley

Small sandwiches will keep fresh for 24 hours if wrapped in plastic wrap and stored in the refrigerator

Spread one slice of bread with butter, and the other with cream cheese. Add little dabs of Marmite to the buttered piece, if you like it; otherwise sprinkle with salt. Lay the lettuce leaves on a chopping board and cut them across in thick (1-inch/2.5 cm) strips. Lay them on one of the slices of bread and cover with the scallions, which you have sliced thin. Pinch the watercress leaves off the stalks and lay them over the scallions. Do the same with the parsley, or chop it coarsely if you prefer, and scatter over the watercress. Top with the second piece of bread and press gently together. Cut in half and wrap in plastic wrap; put in the refrigerator until ready to leave home. This goes well with an apple and a carton of cold milk for solitary picnics, riverside excursions, or boating trips.

Sausage Sandwich

Serves 1
1 large pork dinner sausage, or 2 small sausages
Butter
1 thick wedge French bread, or 2 slices white bread
A little mustard (optional)

Draining on absorbent paper improves most fried foods

Fry the sausage(s) until brown and cooked through; drain on paper towels. When cool, cut in half lengthwise. Butter the bread and lay the sausage halves on one piece. Dab with mustard if you like it, make into a sandwich, and wrap in aluminum foil.

60

Potted Shrimp Sandwich

Serves 1
4 tablespoons (60 g)
  potted shrimp
2 slices fresh whole wheat
  bread
Butter
A squeeze of lemon juice

Spread the bread with butter, then pile the shrimp on one slice, discarding their solidified butter. Squeeze a few drops lemon juice over them, then cover with the second slice to make a sandwich. Squeeze together gently and cut off the crusts. If taking on a picnic, wrap in aluminum foil or plastic wrap. This makes just about the most delicious sandwich you can imagine.

Toad Hall Steak Sandwich

Serves 1

1 rump or sirloin steak,
  6–8 ounces
1 thick wedge French bread,
  or 2 slices white bread

A pinch of salt
A little French mustard
  (optional)
A few sprigs watercress

This is an expensive sandwich to make, so be sure that you use fresh (preferably freshly sliced) bread

Broil the steak under the preheated broiler until medium well done. (It should still be pink in the middle.) Leave for an hour to cool. Butter the bread, and cut the steak in diagonal slices about ¼ inch (6 mm) thick, being careful to catch any juices that run out. Lay the slices of meat on one piece of bread and pour the juices over them. Sprinkle with salt, dab with mustard if you like it, and lay the sprigs of watercress on top. Cover with the second piece of bread and press together. Wrap in aluminum foil if taking on a picnic. If using ordinary white bread, be sure it is thick-cut; don't waste a good steak on thin-sliced bread.

Stuffed Eggs

Serves 4–6
6 large eggs
2 tablespoons heavy cream or (preferably) sour cream
Salt and freshly ground black pepper to taste
4 tablespoons chopped fresh chives

Put the eggs in lightly salted cold water and bring slowly to a boil. Lower heat and simmer gently for 12 minutes, then lift them out with a slotted spoon and drop into a bowl of cold water. When they have cooled, shell them and cut in half, either through the middle, if taking on a picnic, or lengthwise, if to be eaten at home. Scoop out the yolks with a small teaspoon and put them into a bowl. Mash them with a fork, adding the fresh or sour cream, salt and pepper, and chopped chives. Spoon back into the whites, doming them up. If taking on a picnic, pack them standing upright in two egg boxes; otherwise lay them on a dish lined with lettuce leaves. Serves 4–6 as an appetizer or as part of a picnic.

The Mole took out all the mysterious packets one by one and arranged their contents in due order, still gasping, "O my! O my!" at each fresh revelation.

River-Banker's Lunch

Serves 1

A wedge of fresh French bread, served with butter, a piece of Cheddar or other cheese, and some chutney (see recipe for Tomato Chutney, page 49).

Hard-Cooked Eggs with Nutty Spice Island Mixture

Do remember that eggs are best used at room temperature

Serves 1
2 hard-cooked eggs
Nutty Spice Island Mixture (see page 48)
Buttered whole wheat bread

Put the eggs in cold water, add a little salt, and bring to a boil. Simmer for 12 minutes, then remove the eggs and drop them into a bowl of cold water. Leave until cold. Pack a couple of tablespoons of the Nutty Spice Island Mixture in a small plastic carton, or in a twist of aluminum foil. Make a whole-wheat-bread-and-butter sandwich to eat with the eggs. Shell the eggs and dip them in the spice mixture. Alternatively, make into a sandwich with the bread and butter.

"There's cold chicken inside it," replied the Rat briefly; "coldtonguecoldham coldbeefpickledgherkins saladfrenchrollscressand widgespottedmeatginger beerlemonadesodawater—" "O stop, stop," cried the Mole in ecstasies: "This is too much!"

Sausage Rolls

Makes 6 large sausage rolls (serves 6)
1 pound (450 g) pastry, frozen or homemade

Ingredients for pastry, if made at home:
2½ cups (275 g) all-purpose flour
6 tablespoons (90 g) butter
4 tablespoons (60 g) lard
A pinch of salt
A little ice water

6 large pork dinner sausages
1 egg yolk
1 tablespoon milk

Try to wash the pans and utensils as you go along

Start the pastry an hour ahead. If frozen, leave to thaw. If making by hand, sift the flour into a large bowl and add a pinch of salt. Cut the butter and lard into small bits and mix into the flour with the blade of a knife. Using your fingertips, rub the fats and flour together lightly, until the mixture resembles coarse bread crumbs. Then pour in a little ice water very gradually, mixing all the time with the knife blade, until the dough is moist enough to cling together. Gather it together, wrap in plastic wrap, and chill for 30 minutes in the refrigerator. If using a food processor, simply put the sifted flour and the bits of fat in the container and process until mixed, not too long. Then pour the water very slowly through the hole in the lid, while continuing to process, until the dough forms a large ball. Turn out, wrap in plastic wrap, and chill as described above. Preheat the oven to 425° F (220° C), and then cook the sausages in a little fat in a frying pan or skillet, or follow the package directions. Turn them over until they are nicely browned all over, but only cook about half as long as usual. (They will finish cooking in the oven.) Drain them on paper towels. When ready to use, roll out the pastry into a long strip about 5 inches (12.5 cm) wide and ⅛ inch (3 mm) thick. Lay a sausage on it, folding over the pastry to make a narrow overlap, then cut and trim. Seal the edges by dampening the inner sides and pressing them gently together. Brush with egg yolk beaten together with milk. Lay the rolls on an oiled baking sheet and bake for 20 minutes in the hot oven. Take out of the oven and leave to cool for 5 minutes, then wrap in aluminum foil (if taking on a picnic). If eating at home, serve hot or warm. They can also be left to cool and reheated, or eaten cold.

"All complete!" said the Toad triumphantly, pulling open a locker. "You see—biscuits, potted lobster, sardines— everything you can possibly want. Soda-water here—baccy there—letter-paper, bacon, jam, cards and dominoes . . ."

Leafy Summer Lettuce Snacks

Serves 4

8 Frankfurters, cooked chicken legs, or wedges of hard
    cheese (Emmenthal, Gruyère, or Cheddar)
Inner leaves of a crisp lettuce, romaine or iceberg
A little mustard, mild relish, or chutney

Time should be
allowed for the
frankfurters to cool

If using frankfurters, soften them by putting them in a pan
of nearly boiling water and removing from the heat. Cover
the pan and leave for 10 minutes. Remove from the water
and leave to cool, then lay each one in a lettuce leaf. Dab
with mustard or mild relish, then roll them up and lay in a
damp dish towel or in a plastic box, or in aluminum foil. If
using chicken legs, these are best broiled (see recipe for
River-Banker's Broiled Chicken, page 83), although baked
chicken legs are good, too. Dab them with chutney or
relish and roll up as above. If using cheese, remove the rind
and cut in long wedges. Dab with chutney and roll up as
above.

*"It is a splendid day.
Come for a row, or a
stroll along the hedges,
or a picnic in the woods,
or something."*

Cornish Pasties

Take the meat out
of the refrigerator an
hour before
cooking it

Makes 4 pasties (serves 4)
1 pound (450 g) pastry, frozen or homemade
    (if homemade, see page 72 for ingredients)
6 ounces (175 g) broiling steak (rump or sirloin)
6 tablespoons (75 g) peeled, cubed potato
2 tablespoons (30 g) chopped onion
Salt and freshly ground black pepper to taste
1 egg yolk
1 tablespoon milk

Preheat the oven to 400° F (205° C). If using frozen
pastry, follow instructions on package. If making it at
home, see recipe for Sausage Rolls, page 64, for
instructions. While it thaws (if frozen), or chills (if
homemade), make the filling. Cut the steak into small
cubes, and cut the peeled potato into similar-sized cubes.
Chop the onion fine, and mix all together in a bowl,
adding plenty of salt and pepper, and 1 teaspoon water.
Roll out the pastry into a square about ⅛ inch (3 mm)
thick. Using a large saucer as a guide, cut 4 circles about 6
inches (15 cm) across. Divide the filling into 4 parts, and
lay one on one half of each circle. Fold the other half
across, and seal by dampening the inner side of the edges
and pinching together. Make crimped edges with the edge
of a narrow wooden spoon, or a pencil. Brush them over
with the egg yolk beaten with the milk. Lay the pasties on
an oiled baking sheet and bake in the hot oven for 15
minutes. Then turn down the oven to 250° F (125° C) and
cook for a further 45 minutes. If taking on a picnic, cool
pasties for 5 minutes after taking out of the oven, then
wrap in aluminum foil. If eating at home, serve hot or
warm. They can also be reheated, or eaten cold.

Hot Meat Pasties

Makes 4 pasties (serves 4)
1 medium carrot
Salt and freshly ground
    pepper to taste
1 medium onion
3 tablespoons (45 g) butter
1 pound 2 ounces (500 g)
    ground beef (uncooked)
½ tablespoon all-purpose flour

1½–2 tablespoons chopped
    fresh parsley
12 ounces (350 g) pastry,
    frozen or homemade (if
    homemade, see page 64
    for ingredients)
1 egg yolk
1 tablespoon milk

If you haven't got the right equipment, always try to think of an alternative. This also applies to ingredients

Preheat the oven to 350° F (175° C). Peel or scrape and chop the carrot and put it in a small pan with enough water to just cover; add a pinch of salt and bring to the boil. Cook for 5 minutes, then put aside. Chop the onion and fry gently in the butter, in a frying pan or skillet, until pale golden. Add the ground meat and brown lightly, stirring often. Then add the flour, stirring until blended. Pour on the carrot and its cooking water, made up to ⅔ cup (160 ml) with more water, and stir again. Bring to a boil, stirring, and cook gently for 5 minutes, until most of the liquid has boiled away and thickened into a sauce. Add salt and pepper to taste, stir in the chopped parsley, and leave to cool. If using frozen pastry, follow the package directions. If making it at home, follow instructions on page 64. Roll out the pastry and use two-thirds of it to line 4 small patty tins; fill them with the cooled ground meat, heaping it up generously. Cover with the remaining pastry and trim the edges. Dampen the inner edges of the 2 layers and pinch them together to seal. Make little notches in the edge, using the handle of a fork. Brush the tops with egg yolk lightly beaten with the milk, then lay them on a baking sheet. If you haven't got any patty tins, cut the rolled-out pastry into 4 squares. Divide the meat mixture in 4 and put in the center of each square. Then dampen the edges of each square and fold over to form a triangle.

Pinch the edges firmly together to seal, make little notches in the edge, and brush the tops with the lightly beaten egg yolk and milk.

Bake in the oven for 20 minutes, until they are golden brown. They can be eaten immediately, kept hot, left to cool and reheated, or eaten cold. If taking on a picnic, allow them to cool for 5 minutes, then wrap them in aluminum foil and pack, ideally in an insulated bag.

"I suppose we ought to be moving. I wonder which of us had better pack the luncheon-basket?" He did not speak as if he was frightfully eager for the treat.

Rabbit Pasties

Makes 10 pasties

About 1 pound 2 ounces (500 g) rabbit pieces, or 8 ounces (225 g) boneless rabbit

1 medium onion

1 medium carrot

1 leek

1 rib celery

½ bay leaf

Salt and freshly ground black pepper to taste

3 tablespoons (45 g) butter

2 tablespoons all-purpose flour

2 tablespoons chopped fresh parsley

1½ pounds (675 g) pastry, homemade or frozen (if homemade, see page 64 for ingredients)

1 egg yolk

1 tablespoon milk

The oven should be preheated before the pasties are put in it. This will take about 15 minutes

Put the rabbit pieces, or the boneless rabbit, in a flameproof casserole and add the whole peeled and trimmed vegetables, bay leaf, and salt and pepper. Just cover with cold water, bring to a boil, and simmer for 1½ hours for rabbit pieces or 1 hour for boneless rabbit. Lift out the rabbit, onion, carrot, and leek; discard the celery and bay leaf and strain the stock. Cut the meat off the bones, if using joints, and chop the flesh in small cubes. Dice the cooked vegetables. Melt the butter in a saucepan over medium heat, add the flour, and cook for 1 minute, stirring constantly. Add 1¼ cups (300 ml) of the strained stock, little by little, off the heat, and stir until each addition is blended. When all is well mixed, replace the pan over low heat and stir constantly until thickened. Simmer gently for 3 minutes, adding salt and pepper to taste. Stir in the chopped rabbit and vegetables, add the parsley, then leave to cool. Heat the oven to 400° F (205°

C). If using frozen pastry, follow package directions. If making it at home, follow directions on page 64. Roll out the pastry into a square about ⅛ inch (3 mm) thick. Using a saucer as a guide, cut 10 circles about 5 inches (12.5 cm) across. Lay some of the filling on half of each circle, then fold the other half across to make a semicircle, like a small Cornish pasty. Dampen the inner edges and pinch together to seal, crimping the edges with the side of a fork. Brush with the egg yolk beaten with the milk and lay on an oiled baking sheet. Bake for 20 minutes, or until golden brown. Serve hot, or warm. They can also be reheated, or kept warm for taking on a picnic by wrapping in aluminum foil. This recipe makes 10 pasties; if you like, half can be frozen (after cooling), and kept for a later date. Chicken can be substituted for rabbit, if preferred.

"O, never mind about the washing," said Toad, not liking the subject. "Try and fix your mind on that rabbit. A nice fat young rabbit, I'll be bound. Got any onions?"

Easy Meat Loaf

Serves 4–5

2 pounds (900 g) ground beef
1 large onion, peeled
⅔ cup (160 ml) chopped fresh parsley
Salt and freshly ground black pepper to taste
1½ cups (350 g) canned tomatoes
A pinch of sugar

Preheat the oven to 350° F (175° C). Put the beef in a large bowl. Cut the onion in half, lay each half cut side down, and slice downward thinly. Chop the slices and mix with the ground beef, adding the chopped parsley and salt and black pepper. Spread the mixture in a shallow baking pan; ideally, this should be square and about 1¼ inches (3 cm) deep. Make the top even by smoothing it out with a spatula. Put the canned tomatoes in a bowl with their juice and chop them coarsely with the edge of the spatula, adding salt and black pepper to taste and a pinch of sugar. Pour this over the meat and bake in the oven for 1 hour. When it is cooked, the meat will have shrunk away from the sides of the pan, which will have filled up with gravy. Extract this with a bulb-type baster, if you have one, or pour carefully into a small jug. Serve the meat loaf straight from the pan, cut into squares, accompanied by its own gravy, boiled potatoes, and a green salad. This is also good cold, and can be taken on a picnic. Simply extract the juice as above and leave the meat to get cold. It will then become quite firm, almost hard enough to eat with the fingers. Wrap the whole pan in aluminum foil. To serve, cut the meat loaf in strips and eat wrapped in lettuce leaves. Keep the gravy for another dish, possibly to add to a spaghetti sauce.

Do not be put off if you haven't got a square pan; a round one measuring roughly 10 inches (25 cm) across will do just as well, or anything of similar size

"Toad's out, for one," replied the Otter. "In his brand-new wager-boat; new togs, new everything!" . . . "Such a good fellow, too," remarked the Otter reflectively. "But no stability—especially in a boat!"

Very Easy Flapjacks

Makes 12 large flapjacks
6 tablespoons (90 g) butter
6 tablespoons (90 g) soft brown sugar
3 tablespoons (45 g) syrup
4 ounces (120 g) Rice Krispies or corn flakes (about 4
    cups)
2¼ tablespoons (30–60 g) chopped nuts, or 2 tablespoons
    chopped plain chocolate, drinking chocolate, or cocoa

Put the butter, sugar, and syrup in a saucepan and heat gently. When the butter has melted, stir together to mix well and add the Rice Krispies (or corn flakes). Stir for a moment or two until very well mixed, adding the nuts if used, then spoon into a greased pan, preferably a shallow square one, to make a cake about ¾ inch (2 cm) thick. Leave to cool for about 2 hours, then cut into rectangular strips. Alternatively, shape into round balls, placing on a greased cookie sheet, or in little paper baking cups.

    Variation: Omit the nuts, and add 2 tablespoons chopped plain chocolate—or drinking chocolate, or cocoa—to the butter, sugar, and syrup in the saucepan. Make sure the chocolate melts before adding the Rice Krispies or corn flakes. The chocolate version is best made in round balls. The rectangular shape, without chocolate, is best for picnics, as it is easier to wrap; the round ones should be made only for eating at home.

Chocolate becomes lumpy if it is overheated

Flapjacks

Makes 8
6 tablespoons (90 g) butter
6 tablespoons (90 g) soft brown sugar
3 tablespoons (45 g) syrup
4 ounces (120 g) old-fashioned breakfast oats

Preheat the oven to 350° F (175° C). Put the butter, sugar, and syrup in a saucepan and heat gently. When the butter has melted, stir to mix well, then remove from the heat and stir in the oats. When well mixed, spoon the mixture into a shallow baking pan about 6 inches (15 cm) square, well greased with butter. Spread the mixture evenly, smoothing it with a spatula. Bake for 15 minutes. Leave to cool in the pan, then cut in squares or rectangles and lift out carefully. If taking on a picnic, wrap in aluminum foil.

Everywhere piles and bundles of wheat, oats, barley, beech-mast, and nuts, lay about ready for transport.

5

Food for Celebrations

These are things for parties, perhaps for someone's birthday, or celebrations like the Banquet after the Weasels have been vanquished. Most of them are for puddings and cakes; some are more difficult than others. Some are for ice cream; if you have an ice cream maker this is no problem. They can be made quite well in ice trays, but make sure that it's all right to commandeer these; the atmosphere in my house wouldn't be very happy if I found I couldn't have any ice with my drink, especially in the hot weather when one is most likely to be making ice cream. . . . There are also some recipes for dinner parties, such as Veal Stroganoff, Nut Grove Ice Cream, and Snowfalls in Dark Woods.

Cauliflower, Egg, and Shrimp Mayonnaise

Serves 3—4

1 pound (450 g) unshelled
    cooked shrimp, or ½ pound
    (225 g) shelled cooked
    shrimp, fresh or frozen
1 small cauliflower
4 hard-cooked eggs
4 tablespoons (60 ml)
    mayonnaise, homemade
    or bought

4 tablespoons (60 ml)
    plain yogurt
½ teaspoon Dijon mustard
½ tablespoon lemon juice
2—3 dashes Tabasco
    (optional)
2 tablespoons chopped
    fresh parsley
Salt to taste

Many dishes, including this one, are improved by being served at room temperature. Overchilling can spoil flavor

If using unshelled shrimp (these have the most flavor), shell them and put aside. If using frozen shrimp, tip onto a plate and leave to thaw for 2—3 hours; drain off the water before using. Wash the cauliflower carefully and cut into flowerets, using a small knife. Discard the leaves and stalk. Bring a pan of lightly salted water to the boil over medium heat, throw in the cauliflower sprigs, and bring back to the boil. Boil steadily, uncovered, for about 8 minutes. Using a sharp skewer or thin fork, test the cauliflower to see if it is cooked; it should be soft but still firm. Tip into a colander or large strainer over the sink. Leave for 10—15 minutes to cool, then tip into a large bowl. Shell the eggs and cut in quarters, then cut each quarter across in half, so that each egg makes 8 neat chunks. Make the sauce by mixing the mayonnaise with the yogurt. Add the mustard and lemon juice, and a few drops of Tabasco if you like a hot taste. Spoon half the sauce over the cauliflower and mix gently, trying not to break it. (If it falls apart, it has been overcooked; remember to cook it less next time.) Scatter the shelled shrimp and chopped egg over the cauliflower; add the rest of the sauce and mix again, adding half the chopped parsley. Tip onto a clean platter and scatter the remaining parsley over all. Serve at room temperature. Serves 4 as an appetizer, or 3 as a light main dish.

Eggs in Onion Sauce

Try to use a
standard measuring
cup and a set of
measuring spoons

Serves 3—4

2 cups (475 ml) milk
½ small onion, stuck with a
  whole clove
¼ bay leaf
Salt and freshly ground black
  pepper to taste
6 eggs

1½ pounds (675 g) onions
3 tablespoons (45 g) butter
2 tablespoons all-purpose flour
2 tablespoons grated hard
  cheese: Cheddar, Gruyère,
  or Emmenthal

Put the milk in a small pan with the onion stuck with the clove, bay leaf, a pinch of salt, and a little coarse black pepper. Heat slowly; when it starts to boil, remove from the heat, cover the pan, and leave for 20 minutes to infuse the flavors. Then pour it through a strainer. Peel the onions and slice thickly and put in a pan with lightly salted water to barely cover. Bring to a boil and simmer for about 15 minutes, or until soft, then drain in a colander or large strainer over the sink. Cover the eggs with cold water, add a little salt, and bring slowly to a boil; cook for 12 minutes, then lift them out and plunge into cold water. When they have cooled enough to handle, remove the shells and cut them in halves or quarters. Preheat the oven to 325° F (160° C). Melt the butter, stir in the flour, and cook for 1 minute. Then pour on the strained milk gradually, stirring until smooth, and cook for 3 minutes, adding salt and pepper if needed. When the sauce is smooth and well seasoned, stir in the drained sliced onions, and finally fold in the eggs gently. Pour into a shallow buttered dish and scatter the grated cheese over the top. Heat for 20 minutes in the oven, then brown briefly under the broiler. Serves 4 as an appetizer for a party, or 3 as a main dish, with a tossed green salad.

Mole trudged off to the nearest village, a long way off, for milk and eggs and various necessaries the Toad had, of course, forgotten to provide.

79

Raw Vegetables with Dipping Sauce

Serves 4–5

Scallions, carrots, celery, radishes, cucumber, baby white
    turnips, green pepper, cauliflower, broccoli, etc.

Dipping sauce:

⅔ cup (160 ml) mayonnaise, homemade or bought

⅔ cup (160 ml) sour cream or plain yogurt

2 tablespoons tomato puree, *or* 2 teaspoons tomato
    ketchup

A squeeze of lemon juice, *or* a dash of Tabasco

Have about 3 different vegetables, cleaned and trimmed.
Leave scallions and radishes whole after trimming, cut
carrots and celery in strips, peel cucumber and cut in
wedges, pare turnips and cut in slices. If there is time, chill
for an hour before serving. Make the dip by mixing the
mayonnaise with the sour cream or yogurt, and stirring in
the tomato puree or ketchup. Add a dash of lemon or
Tabasco to taste. I think the best combination is
mayonnaise with sour cream, tomato puree, and Tabasco.
Serve the vegetables prettily arranged on a platter or in a
shallow bowl, with some ice cubes among them. Pass the
dip in a bowl. This is easily made in double quantities for a
party. DO use a good mayonnaise, if bought.

He got out the luncheon-basket and packed a simple meal, in which, remembering the stranger's origin and preferences, he took care to include a yard of long French loaf, a sausage out of which the garlic sang, some cheese which lay down and cried, and a long-necked straw-covered flask containing bottled sunshine shed and garnered on far Southern slopes.

80

Veal Stroganoff

It is particularly
important when
making this dish to
have all the
equipment and
ingredients ready
before starting

Serves 3—4

12 ounces (350 g) veal scallops or lean boneless pork (cut
    from pork loin)
½ cup (120 g) chopped onion (about 1 medium onion)
½ cup (100 g) sliced mushrooms, caps only
1 cup (225 g) peeled, seeded, and chopped tomatoes
About 8 tablespoons (120 g) butter
Salt and freshly ground black pepper to taste
⅔ cup (160 ml) sour cream

This dish must be cooked and served very quickly, so have
everything prepared before you start. If using veal scallops,
cut them in strips about 2 × 1 inch (5 × 2.5 cm). If using
boneless pork, cut it in slices about ⅜ inch (1 cm) thick,
then cut each slice in half lengthwise. Prepare the
vegetables, keeping them in separate piles. Heat 2
tablespoons of the butter in a frying pan or skillet over low
heat, and cook the onions slowly until they are soft,
without allowing them to brown. Tip them into a bowl,
wipe out the pan, and heat another 2 tablespoons of the
butter. Before it gets too hot, put in the sliced mushrooms
and cook briefly, until they soften and wilt. Add them to
the onions, wipe out the pan, and heat another 2
tablespoons butter. Add the chopped tomatoes and cook
very briefly indeed, just until they soften, then add them to
the other cooked vegetables. Wipe out the pan once more,
reheat with the remaining butter, and cook the little strips
of meat quickly, until they have browned all over, turning
them often, and testing one to make sure it is cooked
through. Do not cook more than a few moments or they
will toughen. As soon as they are ready, tip the vegetables
on top of them and mix quickly, adding the sour cream,
and salt and pepper to taste. Toss for a couple of moments,
then tip into a serving dish. Serve with a potato puree
(page 91) or noodles, or rice, with a tossed green salad.

Red Lion Spare Ribs with Barbecue Sauce

Serves 2–4

Barbecue sauce:

1 large onion
3 tablespoons (45 ml) olive oil
1 (6-ounce/90 ml) can tomato puree
1½ tablespoons cider vinegar or wine vinegar
⅔ cup (160 ml) chicken stock, made with ¼ bouillon cube
1½ tablespoons honey or syrup
½ teaspoon Dijon mustard
1 small clove garlic, crushed (optional)
Salt and freshly ground black pepper to taste
½ teaspoon dried oregano (optional)
A dash of Tabasco (optional)
2 pounds (900 g) pork spare ribs

The sauce for this recipe should be made in advance, preferably the day before

Make the sauce some hours in advance, or the day before. Peel and chop the onion and cook slowly in the oil in a broad, heavy pan. While it is cooking, mix the tomato puree with the vinegar to make a paste. When the onions are soft—they should not become brown if you keep the heat low—stir in the paste. Mix well, then add the stock. Then stir in the honey or syrup, mustard, and crushed garlic. Stir in the salt and black pepper, and a little dried oregano if you have it. Cook gently for 15 minutes, stirring often; if it gets too thick, add a drop of hot water. When it has finished cooking it should be quite thick and jammy, but without sticking to the pan. Turn off the heat, add a dash of Tabasco if you like it, and leave to cool. An hour or two before cooking the ribs, lay them out in a flat dish and brush them with the sauce. Let stand for 1–2 hours, then lay them in a baking pan lined with aluminum foil, spreading them out as much as possible. Heat the oven to 450° F (230° C). Brush the ribs with more sauce and bake for 1 hour on the top shelf of the oven. Turn them over

He was satisfied to jog in the sun, taking advantage of any by-ways and bridle-paths, and trying to forget how very long it was since he had had a square meal.

and move them around once or twice during the cooking, brushing with more sauce if necessary. Get an adult to help you do this, as it is very easy to burn your fingers. Put any remaining sauce in the blender and puree, then pour into a small bowl. Serve the ribs piled on a flat dish, passing the extra sauce separately. Eat them with your fingers, dipping them in the sauce. Serves 4 as an appetizer, or 2 as a main dish.

River-Banker's Broiled Chicken

Serves 2—4
1—2 very small chickens (poussins) or Rock Cornish game
    hens, cut in half
Dijon mustard
Olive oil
Lemon juice

To cut down on the cleaning up, cover the bottom of the broiler pan with aluminum foil

Lay the chicken halves skin side up on a platter and spread a layer of Dijon mustard all over the top surface. Dribble a little olive oil over them, and some lemon juice, allowing ½ lemon per chicken. Leave for an hour before cooking, if possible. Heat the broiler, and when it is very hot, put the chickens under it, quite close to the heat. Cook for 5 minutes, then move them a little farther away (or lower the heat), and cook for another 5 minutes. Then remove them from the broiler, turn them over, and baste with olive oil and lemon juice, omitting the mustard. Put back under the broiler, not too close, and cook for 10 minutes. When the time is up, the chickens should be crisp and almost slightly burned on the outside, especially the skin, and white and tender in the center. Serve as soon as possible after cooking, with a tossed green salad. Allow half a chicken per person.

Chicken Pie

Serves 5–6

1 large roasting chicken
    (4–4½ pounds / 1.8–2 kg)
1 large onion, peeled
1 large carrot, peeled or
    scraped
1 rib celery
1 bay leaf
Salt and freshly ground black
    pepper to taste
½ teaspoon black peppercorns
6 small leeks, trimmed and
    well washed
6 small carrots, scraped

½ cup (120 g) shelled
    green peas, fresh or frozen
3 tablespoons (45 g) butter
2 tablespoons all-purpose flour
⅔ cup (160 ml) light cream
2 tablespoons chopped fresh
    parsley
12 ounces (350 g) pastry,
    homemade (see page 64)
    or frozen
1 egg yolk
1 tablespoon milk

The faster stock is boiled, the quicker it will reduce in quantity

Put the chicken in a deep pot. Add the onion, carrot, and celery, cut into large pieces, also the bay leaf, 1 tablespoon salt, and ½ teaspoon black peppercorns. Barely cover with hot water and bring to a boil over medium heat. Lower the heat, cover the pot, and simmer for 1¼ hours. Lift out the chicken and boil the stock, uncovered, for about 5 minutes to reduce the quantity and concentrate the flavor; you need only about 2 cups (475 ml). Then discard the flavoring vegetables and bay leaf, and strain the stock. Preheat the oven to 400° F (205° C). If making your own pastry, do so now (see page 64 for instructions), and chill for 30 minutes. If using frozen pastry, follow package directions. Cook the small leeks and carrots, whole, in separate saucepans. Cover with lightly salted water and boil until just tender; drain well. Blanch the peas for 2 minutes in boiling water; drain. Carve the chicken in neat pieces, discarding the skin, and lay the pieces in a shallow pie dish. Lay the poached vegetables over and among them. Heat the butter in a saucepan over medium heat, add the flour, and cook for 1 minute, stirring constantly. Measure 2 cups

(475 ml) of the strained stock and add gradually, off the heat, stirring in each addition. Replace over the heat and stir for 3 minutes, until thickened and smooth. Add the cream, salt and pepper to taste, and finally the chopped parsley. Pour over the chicken in its dish. Roll out the pastry, cut a strip about ½ inch (1.3 cm) broad, and lay it around the edges of the dish, which you have dampened. Press it down so that it sticks, then dampen the top edge; lay the pastry lid over this and press the edges gently to seal. Crimp the edges and decorate with pastry trimmings if you like. Beat the egg yolk with the milk, then brush the pastry all over with this glaze. Bake for 15 minutes, then turn down the oven to 350° F (175° C) and bake for another 15 minutes. This pie is excellent hot or cold, and can also be reheated. Serve with new potatoes, or a potato puree (see page 91) and green beans, broccoli, or cauliflower.

Most and best of all, he had had a substantial meal, hot and nourishing, and felt big, strong, and careless and self-confident . . . "Ho, ho!" he said to himself as he marched along with his chin in the air, "what a clever Toad I am!"

Steak and Kidney Pie

Serves 4–6

1½ pounds (675 g) chuck steak
½ pound (225 g) beef kidney
Seasoned flour
3 tablespoons (45 g) beef drippings, or other fat
2 onions, peeled and sliced
2 carrots, peeled or scraped and sliced
Salt and freshly ground black pepper to taste
1⅔ cups (400 ml) beef stock, made with a bouillon cube
Suet pastry:
2 cups (225 g) self-rising flour
A pinch of salt
¼ pound (120 g) shredded suet

Take the meat out of the refrigerator an hour before cooking it

Preheat the oven to 300° F (150° C). Cut the meat in small neat cubes and dip them in seasoned flour (plain flour with salt and pepper added). Shake off any excess. Heat the drippings (or other fat) in a flameproof casserole and cook the onions for a few moments, stirring them until they start to soften. Add the carrots and cook gently, all together, until they are lightly colored. Then push the vegetables to the side of the pan and put in the beef steak and kidney, stirring to brown it evenly all over. When all is nicely colored and well mixed, heat the stock and add, stirring until blended with the flour. Add more salt and pepper, cover the casserole, and cook gently for 2 hours in the oven. Just before the time is up, make the pastry. (Suet pastry does not need to rest before using; it must be used straight away.) Sift the flour with the salt into a large bowl. Add the suet and mix with your fingertips. Add just enough cold water to make it all cling together, mixing it with the blade of a knife. Form into a ball, turn out, and knead briefly, just once or twice. Roll out rather thicker than if it were flaky pastry—about ½ inch (1.3 cm) is right. When the beef has finished cooking, take it out of the oven and transfer the contents of the casserole to a pie dish. Cut 4 long strips of pastry about 1 inch (2.5 cm) thick, and press them over the dampened rim of the dish, to make a firm base to hold the pastry lid. Then dampen the upper surface of the pastry rim and lay the lid over it, pressing down firmly to seal. Trim the edges with a knife and crimp the edges. Raise the oven temperature to 375° F (190° C). Bake for 30–40 minutes, or until a golden brown. This pie is good served with a puree of potatoes (see page 91), and boiled leeks and carrots.

When supper was really finished at last, and each animal felt that his skin was now as tight as was decently safe, and that by this time he didn't care a thing for anybody or anything, they gathered round the glowing embers of the great wood fire, and thought how jolly it was to be sitting up so late, and so independent and so full.

Game Pie

Serves 8

1 pound (450 g) stewing venison

1 pound (450 g) boneless rabbit

1 pheasant, or 2 grouse, or 2 partridges (stewing birds)

1 onion, peeled and halved

1 carrot, peeled or scraped and halved

1 rib celery, halved

1 bay leaf

3 sprigs parsley

Salt and freshly ground black pepper to taste

8 black peppercorns

8 juniper berries

1 (½-ounce/15 g) envelope gelatin

1 pound (450 g) pastry, homemade (see page 64) or frozen

1 egg yolk

1 tablespoon milk

To lift the pastry from the table to the pie dish, either roll it around the rolling pin or fold it in quarters

Cut the venison into large pieces and put in a heavy pot with the boneless rabbit and the whole birds. Add the halved onion, carrot, and celery, and bay leaf, and the salt and black pepper, and barely cover with hot water. Bring to a boil, skimming off the scum that rises to the surface, lower the heat, cover the pot, and simmer for 2 hours. Lift out the meat and birds, discard the flavoring vegetables and bay leaf, and strain the stock. If using your own pastry, make it while the game is cooking, then chill for 30 minutes before using. If using frozen pastry, follow package directions. Heat the oven to 350° F (175° C). When the meat has cooled enough to handle, cut the venison in small neat slices, chop the rabbit in cubes, and carve the birds, cutting the flesh off the bones into neat fillets. Crush the peppercorns and juniper berries roughly together, either in a mortar, or by wrapping them in the corner of a dish towel and hitting them once or twice with a rolling pin. Take two thirds of the pastry and roll out thinly to line a cake pan with a removable bottom, which you have greased inside with butter. Lay half the sliced venison in the bottom, sprinkle with some of the crushed peppercorns and juniper berries, adding some salt, then make a layer of half the cubed rabbit, more seasonings, then half the game. Continue making alternate layers, seasoning each one, until all the meat is used up. Moisten with 4 tablespoons of the strained game stock, then roll out the remaining pastry to make a lid. Lay it over the pie so that the edges overlap by about ½ inch (1.3 cm), dampen them, pressing together to seal. Trim them, and roll up to make a thick edge. Decorate with the pastry trimmings to make a centerpiece, such as a flower, or 4 pastry leaves, in the center of the pie. Cut around the centerpiece carefully with a small sharp knife, then brush all over with the egg yolk beaten with the milk. Bake for 1 hour. While pie is in the oven, measure the strained stock and add gelatin, allowing 1 envelope to 2½ cups (600 ml) stock. (Dissolve the gelatin in a little of the stock in a cup, standing it in a pan of simmering water, then mix with the rest of the stock and pour through a strainer.) When the pie has finished cooking, take it out of the oven and lift out the pastry centerpiece. Insert a funnel and pour some of the cool stock into the pie, stopping when it is full. A few moments later, you will be able to add some more; continue in this way until the pie will hold no more, or all the stock is finished. Replace the centerpiece and leave to cool. Keep for 24 hours before serving; it can be kept for up to 1 week in the refrigerator. Enough for 8; it is delicious served with a fruit pickle or chutney, and a tossed greed salad.

It was, indeed, the most beautiful stew in the world, being made of partridges, and pheasants, and chickens, and hares and rabbits, and peahens, and guinea-fowls, and one or two other things. Toad took the plate on his lap, almost crying, and stuffed, and stuffed, and stuffed . . . He thought that he had never eaten so good a breakfast in all his life.

Salmon Fish Cakes

Serves 3—4

½ pound (225 g) cooked
    salmon (about 1 cup)
½ pound (225 g) freshly
    boiled potatoes
    (about 1 cup mashed)
6 tablespoons (90 g) butter
Salt and freshly ground black
    pepper to taste

1 egg yolk
2 tablespoons chopped fresh
    parsley
1 egg, beaten
Dry bread crumbs
2 tablespoons vegetable oil

Chopped parsley
will keep fresh for
several days if
stored in an airtight jar
in the refrigerator

This is a good way to use up leftover cold salmon.
Otherwise, buy fresh salmon, or frozen; if buying fresh fish,
the tail end is the most economical piece. Choose a pan to
fit it nicely, cover it with cold water, and bring slowly to
the boil. As soon as it boils, cover the pan, turn off the
heat, and leave until it is cold. (This is a foolproof way of
cooking salmon to eat cold, and works with any size of
fish, so long as the pan fits it reasonably well.) Later, boil
the potatoes and dry out for a moment or two over low
heat. Push through a vegetable mill into a large bowl.
While they are still hot, stir in 4 tablespoons butter cut in
small bits, season with plenty of salt and black pepper, and
stir in the egg yolk. Flake the fish, discarding skin and
bones, and chop it coarsely. Stir it into the potato, beating
with a wooden spoon until thoroughly blended. Stir in the
chopped parsley, and more salt and pepper if needed. The
mixture can be made in advance up to this stage, and left
in the refrigerator for a few hours, or overnight. Just before
cooking, form into round cakes: I like large fish cakes, and
make 4 or 6 depending on the number of people, but it
will make 8 small cakes if you prefer. Dip them first in the
beaten egg, then in the bread crumbs. Heat the remaining
2 tablespoons butter with the oil in a frying pan or skillet
over medium heat and fry the fish cakes for about 4
minutes on each side, until golden brown. Serve large fish
cakes for supper, with green peas or sweet corn; small fish
cakes are delicious for a late breakfast or brunch.

Potato Puree

Serves 5–6

Try to wash the pans and utensils as you go along

2 pounds (900 g) potatoes
¾ cup (200 ml) milk
8 tablespoons (120 g) butter

Salt and freshly ground black
pepper to taste

Peel the potatoes, cutting them in half if they are very large. Put them in a pan and cover with lightly salted cold water; bring to a boil and boil steadily (uncovered), until they are soft when pierced with a thin skewer. Drain thoroughly, then return to the pan and shake over very gentle heat for a minute or two, to drive out the remaining moisture. Tip them into a food mill and stand for a moment while you clean out the pan. Put the milk and butter in a small pan with a pouring lip; add plenty of salt and pepper, remembering that it has to season the mass of potatoes, not just the milk. Put it over a low heat to warm, while you push the potatoes through the food mill into the clean dry pan. Stir the resulting puree over low heat for a few moments to continue the drying-out process, then— when the butter has melted—start to pour in the buttery milk a little at a time, beating in each addition until you have a smooth creamy puree. Tip into a hot dish to serve. If it has to be kept hot for a little, this is best done in the pan. Save a little of the buttery milk and pour over the top of the potato to prevent a skin forming; cover with the lid and leave in a warm place. Just before serving, beat in the remaining liquid and tip into the serving dish. This is delicious with all dishes of meat or fish, and with cold meat. Enough for 5–6, but you can never have too much of it.

Salmon leap on the flood tide, schools of mackerel flash and play past quaysides and foreshores, and by the windows the great vessels glide, night and day, up to their moorings or forth to the open sea.

Snowfalls in Dark Woods

Serves 6

3½ ounces (100 g) bitter (dark) chocolate
4 eggs, separated, at room temperature
3 tablespoons (45 g) superfine sugar, sifted
¾ cup (200 ml) heavy cream, lightly whipped

Preheat the oven to 350° F (175° C). Break the chocolate into squares. Grate 2 of them and set aside; put the rest in a small earthenware bowl and set it over a saucepan containing very hot water. Do not let the bowl touch the water. Keep the water just below boiling point until the chocolate has melted, 8–10 minutes. Then remove the bowl and leave to cool. When the chocolate has reached room temperature or thereabouts, beat the egg yolks in a large bowl, using an electric hand beater or a wire whisk. Add the sifted sugar gradually, continuing to beat, then add the melted chocolate. Wash and dry the beater or whisk, then beat the egg whites in another bowl until they stand in peaks. Fold them into the chocolate mixture. Have a shallow baking pan lined with buttered aluminum foil; a square pan measuring 8 × 8 × 1½ inches (20 × 20 × 4 cm) is ideal, but a round one will do. Tip the chocolate into this and bake in the oven for 15–20 minutes. It is done when it is just firm to the touch in the center, and starting to come away from the sides of the pan. Take out of the oven and leave to cool for 10 minutes, then tip out onto a clean cloth. Peel off the aluminum foil and lay a flat dish over the cake. Turn the whole thing upside down, so that the cake is lying right side up on the plate. (If you use a square tin, you may have trouble finding a plate big enough; a flat board or even a small tray will do just as well.) When it has cooled completely, cover all over with a layer of lightly whipped cream and scatter the grated chocolate over it. Do not chill; serve at room temperature. This makes a lovely dessert for a party, pretty and delicious.

If a recipe calls for a pan to be lined with greased paper or aluminum foil, don't try to save time by skipping this instruction!

92

Millionaire's Bread and Butter Pudding

Setting the dish in a pan of hot, but not boiling, water will prevent the egg and milk mixture from boiling while it is in the oven

Serves 4

1¼ cups (300 ml) milk

⅔ cup (160 ml) light cream

3 eggs

6 tablespoons (90 g) sugar

10—12 slices of a stale French loaf, about ¼ inch (6 mm) thick

About 3 tablespoons (45 g) butter

1 tablespoon raisins (dark or golden)

Vanilla ice cream (optional)

Put the milk and cream in a small pan and heat slowly. Break the eggs into a bowl and add the sugar, and beat until well mixed. When the milk and cream reach boiling point, pour them onto the eggs, continuing to beat. Butter the bread slices and layer them in a buttered ovenproof dish. Scatter the raisins over and among them. Pour the egg and milk mixture over them through a strainer. Preheat oven to 350° F (175° C). Have a baking pan half full of hot water. Put it in the oven and stand the dish in it. Bake for 40 minutes, then take out of the oven and leave to cool for about 30 minutes. For a party, serve warm with vanilla ice cream.

They braced themselves for the last long stretch, the home stretch, the stretch that we know is bound to end, some time, in the rattle of the door latch, the sudden firelight, and the sight of familiar things greeting us as long-absent travellers from far oversea. They plodded along steadily and silently, each of them thinking his own thoughts. The Mole's ran a good deal on supper.

Apples with Chocolate

Serves 4–6
2 pounds (900 g) cooking apples
½ cup (120 g) sugar
¾ cup (200 ml) heavy cream
2 ounces (60 g) dark chocolate

Peel, core, and slice the apples. Put 4 tablespoons water in a heavy saucepan, add the sliced apples and the sugar, and cook gently, covered, until the apples are soft. Remove the lid and stir now and then so that they cook evenly. When they are soft, push them through a medium food mill or coarse sieve. Leave to cool. Spoon the apple puree into a soufflé dish. Whip the cream, stopping just before it becomes too thick, and spoon over the apples. Grate the chocolate onto a plate, then sprinkle over the cream. Chill for 1–2 hours before serving.

It is important not to overwhip cream for recipes calling for it to be half-whipped. If you do, you may find it impossible to fold the cream smoothly into the rest of the ingredients

Baked Bananas

Serves 4
6 bananas
2 tablespoons (30 g) butter,
    plus butter to grease dish
1 orange
1 lemon

1–2 tablespoons rum
    (optional)
1 tablespoon sugar
Light cream

Remember to preheat the oven before starting

Preheat the oven to 350° F (175° C). Peel the bananas and cut them in half lengthwise. Rub a shallow ovenproof dish with butter and lay them in it. Squeeze the juice of the orange and lemon, add rum if desired, and pour over the bananas. Sprinkle with the sugar and dot with the butter, cut in small bits. Bake for 20 minutes. Cool slightly before serving, about 15–20 minutes. Eat with light cream.

Cheesecake

It is always
essential to wear
oven gloves or use
potholders when
taking food out of
a very hot oven

Serves 6

Crust:

6 ounces (175 g) sweetmeal
cookies

3 tablespoons (45 g) butter

1 heaping tablespoon soft
brown sugar

Filling:

1 cup (225 g) superfine sugar

4 tablespoons (60 g) butter,
creamed

2 egg yolks, beaten

⅔ cup (160 ml) heavy cream

2 (8-ounce/227 g) packages
cream cheese, at room
temperature

either 1½ tablespoons lemon
juice *or* grated zest of ½
small orange

First make the crust. Preheat the oven to 350° F (175° C).
Break the cookies into large crumbs. This can be done in a
number of ways: (a) in a food processor; (b) by wrapping
the biscuits in a clean dish towel and crushing them with a
rolling pin, or (c) by simply breaking them up by hand. If
using a food processor, be careful not to overprocess them
until reduced to powder. Put the crumbs in a bowl, melt
the butter in a small saucepan over low heat, and pour it
over them. Add the brown sugar and mix all together well.
Use two thirds of the mixture to line a round baking pan
with a removable bottom, pressing it up the sides as well as
in the bottom. (Ideally, this pan should be about 2 inches
[5 cm] deep, but this is not vital.) Put the remaining
crumbs in another pan. Bake for 8 minutes. Remove the
pans from the oven and leave to cool.

Later, make the filling. If you are using a food processor,
simply put all the ingredients in together and process until
smooth. Otherwise, sift the superfine sugar into a bowl,
and beat into the creamed butter. When they are smoothly
blended, add the beaten egg yolks and the cream and
blend again. Beat the cream cheese separately, in a large
bowl. When it is free from lumps, beat the first mixture
into it. Stir in the lemon juice or grated orange zest, and
pour into the prepared crust. Sprinkle the separately baked
crumbs over. Chill for several hours, preferably overnight,
before serving.

*"Months and months
out of sight of land, and
provisions running short,
and allowanced as to
water, and your mind
communing with the
mighty ocean, and all
that sort of thing?"*

Toad Hall Trifle

Serves 5–6
1 sponge cake, slightly stale, or 24 stale ladyfingers
Juice of 1 large orange (or 5 tablespoons medium-dry
    sherry, Madeira, or Marsala wine)

Homemade custard:
3 egg yolks
4 tablespoons sugar (preferably superfine)
1¼ cups (300 ml) milk

Bird's custard:
1½ tablespoons Bird's dessert powder
1 cup (300 ml) milk
2 tablespoons sugar

½ cup (225 g) raspberries, fresh or frozen, *or* ½ cup (225
    g) raspberry jam
1½ cups (300 ml) heavy cream
About 2 ounces (60 g) dark chocolate

When beating eggs over simmering water, remember that the bottom of the bowl should not touch the water

Cut the sponge cake into thick chunks (or break ladyfingers in half) and use to line a broad, shallow bowl, preferably made of glass. Pour the orange juice (or wine) over them and leave for a little while for the liquid to be absorbed. If using a homemade custard, beat the egg yolks in a earthenware bowl, using an electric hand beater, or a rotary beater, or wire whisk. Shake in the sugar while beating, and continue to beat until you have a smooth, creamy paste. Choose a pan into which the bowl fits nicely, and place it half filled with simmering water on the stove. Heat the milk in a small pan until boiling, then pour it onto the egg yolks, beating constantly. Stand the bowl in the saucepan over the simmering water and continue to stir with a wooden spoon almost constantly for about 8 minutes, by which time the custard should have slightly thickened, so that it coats the back of the wooden spoon

96

lightly when you lift it out. Then stand the bowl in a sink
half full of cold water so that the custard cools, quickly,
stirring every now and then to prevent a skin from forming.
If using Bird's dessert powder, make as usual, following
the instructions on the container, using half the usual
amount of dessert powder and milk. If using raspberry jam,
spread it over the sponge cake now, then pour the cool
custard over them. If using fresh (or frozen) raspberries,
pour the custard over first, then scatter the berries over it.
If possible, stand the bowl in the refrigerator for an hour or
two at this stage. Then whip the cream and spread it over
the berries. If possible, chill again for an hour or two before
serving. Just before serving, scatter chocolate shavings—or
grated chocolate—over the top. This is done by scraping a
small sharp knife over the flat side of a bar of plain
chocolate, making thin, curly shavings. Alternatively, the
chocolate can be simply grated, or you can use chocolate
sprinkles. When made with whole berries, this is a very
delicious dessert for a party.

Some people use alcohol to soak the cake in—I'm sure
Toad did—but I prefer orange juice. If you want to make
it their way, however, simply substitute 5 tablespoons
medium-dry sherry (or Madeira or Marsala) for the orange
juice.

DON'T worry if a homemade custard turns out rather
thin; simply pour it over the cakes a bit at a time, and wait
for them to absorb it before adding more.

*"Perhaps he's not very clever—we can't all be
geniuses; and it may be that he is both boastful
and conceited. But he has got some great
qualities, has Toady."*

Plum Crumble

Serves 4
1 pound (450 g) plums
4 tablespoons (60 ml) orange
  juice
½ cup (60 g) all-purpose
  flour

½ cup (120 g) sugar
½ teaspoon ground cinnamon
  (optional)
A pinch of salt
4 tablespoons (60 g) butter
Cream

Cut the plums in half, remove the pits, then cut each half into square pieces. Put them in an ovenproof dish and pour the orange juice over them. Preheat the oven to 375° F (190° C). Sift the flour into a bowl and stir in the sugar, cinnamon (if used), and salt. Add the butter, cut into small pieces, then lightly rub it into the flour, using your fingertips, until it is evenly mixed, almost like bread crumbs. Spread this mixture over the plums, patting it down firmly so that it covers the whole dish. Bake in the oven for 35–40 minutes, or until golden brown. Let stand for 30 minutes after taking out of the oven before serving, with cream.

Blackberry and Apple Meringue

1 large cooking apple
¼ cup (60 g) granulated
  sugar
1 pound (450 g) blackberries
Juice of ½ lemon

2 egg whites, at room
  temperature
6 tablespoons (90 g)
  superfine sugar
Heavy cream

Preheat the oven to 300° F (150° C). Peel and core the apple and cut in thinnish slices. Put the slices in a pan with 2 tablespoons water and the granulated sugar. Cook gently, covered, for 4 minutes; then add the blackberries. Bring back to simmering point and cook for 1 minute. Remove from the heat and add the lemon juice. Tip into a pie dish. Beat the egg whites until stiff, fold in the superfine sugar, and pile over the fruit, covering the dish entirely. Bake for 30 minutes. Then cool for about 30 minutes before serving, with heavy cream.

Pebbles in a Stream

Serves 4

4 large lemons

4–5 sprigs mint

¾ cup (175 g) sugar

1 (½-ounce / 15 g) envelope
  gelatin

12 large white grapes, or
  24 seedless grapes

Start well ahead to
allow time for the
gelatin to set, either
in the morning for
the evening meal,
or a day ahead for
lunchtime

Pare the rind of 1 lemon and put it in a heatproof
measuring cup. Pick 10 of the larger mint leaves and
reserve; put the sprigs in the cup. Squeeze the juice of all
the lemons and add to the cup. Put the sugar in a saucepan
with ⅔ cup (160 ml) water; bring to a boil and simmer for
a moment or two until the sugar has melted, then pour it
onto the lemon juice and leave until cool. Put ⅓ cup (80
ml) water in a cup and shake in the gelatin. Stand the cup
in a small pan of simmering water; when the gelatin has
melted, remove from the pan and pour it into the lemon
liquid. Make up to 2½ cups (600 ml) with water, if
necessary. When it has completely cooled, line a shallow
rectangular dish with aluminum foil and pour the lemon
liquid into the dish through a strainer. If using large
grapes, peel them, cut in half, and remove the seeds. If
using seedless grapes, simply peel them. Cut the reserved
mint leaves in thin strips lengthwise. Put the grapes into
the gelatin dessert and scatter the strips of mint among
them, so that they look like weeds floating in the water.
Chill in the refrigerator until set.

*"You stayed to
supper, of course?" said
the Mole presently.
"Simply had to," said
the Rat. "They wouldn't
hear of my going before.
You know how kind
they always are."*

Floating Islands

Serves 4–5
3 eggs, separated, at room
   temperature

4 tablespoons (60 g)
   superfine sugar
2 cups (475 ml) milk
½ vanilla bean

The custard can be made in advance, but the poached meringues must be eaten on the day they are made

Beat 2 of the egg whites until stiff, then fold in half the sugar, spoonful by spoonful. Bring some water to a boil in a wide pan. When it reaches the boiling point, lower the heat until it simmers steadily, then drop in spoonfuls of the egg white, using 2 tablespoons. (Fill one with the mixture, then scoop this onto the simmering water with the other.) Poach gently for 3 minutes, then turn them over carefully with a slotted spoon, and poach for a further 2–3 minutes. Only cook a few at a time, giving them plenty of room to swell as they cook. Lift them out with a slotted spoon and lay on a cloth to drain while you poach the next batch. When all are done, and drained, lay them on a flat dish and chill in the refrigerator. Heat the milk with the vanilla bean until almost boiling, then turn off the heat, cover the pan, and leave to infuse the flavor for 10 minutes. Beat the egg yolks with the remaining sugar until pale yellow and creamy, in a basin suitable to set over a pan of water. Reheat the milk until on the point of boiling, and pour through a strainer onto the egg yolks, beating all the time. (The vanilla bean may be washed and dried, and kept for further use.) Stand the bowl with the custard sauce in it over a pan of simmering water and stir constantly, or almost constantly, with a wooden spoon until it has thickened very slightly, just enough to coat the back of the spoon. This may take as much as 12 minutes. Once it has happened, remove from the pan and stand in a sink half-full of icy water. Stir frequently while cooling to prevent a skin from forming. Then chill for 2–3 hours in the refrigerator. To serve, pour the custard sauce into a wide shallow dish and lay the poached meringues on it, like islands floating. Alternatively, it can be served in individual bowls, with 1–2 islands in each one.

Frozen Strawberry Fool

Serves 6
1½ pounds (675 g) strawberries, preferably fresh
6 tablespoons (90 g) superfine sugar
1¼ cups (300 ml) heavy cream

If using a blender or food processor, simply put in the berries with the sugar and puree until mushy. Alternatively, the berries can be first chopped, then pushed through a vegetable mill. If you want to make a fool without any seeds, you must push the berries through a fine nylon sieve, then stir in the cream, which you have lightly whipped, just until thickened without becoming stiff. If you don't mind a few seeds, the cream can be added to the fruit and sugar in the blender or food processor. Pour into a dish and freeze for about 1–1½ hours, until starting to freeze around the edges. Before serving, scrape the frozen parts into the middle, and beat all together. This can be served alone, or with a raspberry sauce (see recipe on page 106). It can be left in its dish, or spooned into glasses. I think this is just as good as ice cream, and much easier to make.

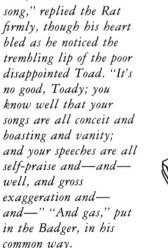

"No, not one little song," replied the Rat firmly, though his heart bled as he noticed the trembling lip of the poor disappointed Toad. "It's no good, Toady; you know well that your songs are all conceit and boasting and vanity; and your speeches are all self-praise and—and—well, and gross exaggeration and—and—" "And gas," put in the Badger, in his common way.

Buried Strawberries

Serves 4–5

1 pound (450 g) strawberries, fresh or frozen
⅔ cup (160 ml) heavy cream
⅔ cup (160 ml) yogurt

1 egg white, at room temperature
2 tablespoons superfine sugar

This dessert is equally delicious made with any other soft fruit, such as raspberries, blueberries, chopped plums or peaches.

If using fresh berries, cut them in halves or quarters, depending on their size. Put them in a dish that they half fill, or individual dishes or bowls, one for each person. (Short, squat tumblers look nice with this dessert, if you have any.) If using frozen strawberries, allow them to thaw, but only just. They should be cold and firm, not mushy. Leave whole and put in a dish or glasses. Whip the cream, beat the yogurt until smooth, and fold it into the cream. Beat the egg white until stiff, and fold into the yogurt-cream mixture. Add the sugar and fold in also. Pile the creamy mixture on top of the berries and chill in the refrigerator for 1 hour before serving. This dessert is equally delicious made with any other soft fruit, i.e. raspberries, blueberries, or chopped pitted plums.

Vanilla Ice Cream

Serves 6

½ vanilla bean, or a few drops vanilla extract
1¼ cups (300 ml) milk
2 eggs plus 2 egg yolks

5 tablespoons (75 g) superfine sugar
1¼ cups (300 ml) heavy cream

It is important not to overwhip cream for recipes calling for it to be half-whipped. If you do, you may find it impossible to fold the cream smoothly into the rest of the ingredients

To make this ice cream, follow the instructions for Nut Grove Ice Cream (page 104), omitting the nuts. A vanilla bean gives a much better flavor than vanilla extract, so use one if you can.

Pearly Dawn Sorbet

Serves 4–6
3 pink grapefruit
4 tablespoons (60 g) sugar
1 egg white, at room temperature

For successfully beaten egg whites, the whisk and bowl must be completely free from grease and water, and the egg whites completely free of yolk

Squeeze the juice of the grapefruit and pour through a strainer. Put the sugar in a small saucepan with ⅔ cup (160 ml) water and bring to a boil. Cook gently for a moment or two, until the sugar has melted, then add to the fruit juice. Pour into ice cube trays—or an ice cream machine if you have one—and freeze for about 1½ hours, or until mushy. Then tip into a blender or food processor—if this is available—and give a quick whiz. Otherwise tip into a bowl and beat by hand. Beat the egg white until stiff, then fold into the fruit mush and tip back into trays (or ice cream machine). Continue to freeze until set. If very hard, take out of the freezer a little before serving, perhaps half an hour, and soften in the refrigerator. Serve in glasses.

Intoxicated with the sparkle, the ripple, the scents and the sounds and the sunlight . . .

Nut Grove Ice Cream

Serves 6
¼ cup (60 g) hazelnuts, almonds, or walnuts
½ cup (120 g) superfine sugar
1¼ cups (300 ml) milk
¼ vanilla bean, or a few drops vanilla extract
2 eggs plus 2 egg yolks
1¼ cups (300 ml) heavy cream

It is very easy to overwhip cream with an electric beater, so if you are using one, watch carefully as you beat

Put the nuts, which must be without skins, in a heavy frying pan or skillet with 2 tablespoons of the sugar. Cook over high heat, stirring constantly, until the sugar turns golden brown and the nuts become caramelized. Immediately as this happens, turn them out onto a cold oiled surface, such as a baking sheet, where they will become hard and crisp as they cool. When they are cold, chop them coarsely by putting in a food processor or blender or wrap in a clean dish towel and crush with a rolling pin. Do not reduce them to a powder; they want to be in smallish, uneven-sized pieces. If using a vanilla bean to flavor the milk, heat the milk with the bean in it slowly, then remove from the heat, cover the pan, and leave for 20 minutes. If using vanilla extract, simply flavor the milk to taste. Beat the eggs in a bowl with the extra yolks, adding the remaining sugar. Reheat (or heat) the flavored milk until almost boiling and pour it onto the eggs, continuing to beat. Stand the bowl over a saucepan of simmering water and stir gently until it has thickened slightly; this may take some 8 minutes. It will never become very thick, but it will just start to coat the back of a wooden spoon, and will thicken further on cooling. When this stage is reached, stand the bowl in a sink half full of cold water and stir often to prevent a skin from forming while it cools. When quite cool, beat the cream until half-whipped, stopping just before it becomes really thick, and fold into the custard. If you let it become really thick, it will be difficult to fold it in evenly; this does not really matter if you have an ice cream machine, but if you are freezing this in ice cube trays it is important to get a smooth consistency. Pour it into ice cube trays, or an ice cream machine if you have one, and freeze for about 1½ hours, until half-frozen. Then turn out into a bowl, beat again if using ice cube trays—this is not necessary if using a machine—then fold in the broken nuts. Pour back into trays or machine, and continue freezing until set. Coarse brown breadcrumbs, fried in butter and sugar until crisp, can be used instead of the nuts.

"Oo-ray-oo-ray-oo-ray-ooray!" they heard, and the stamping of little feet on the floor, and the clinking of glasses as little fists pounded on the table. "What a time they're having!" said the Badger. "Come on!"

Raspberry Sauce

Serves 6
1 cup (225 g) raspberries, fresh or frozen
2 tablespoons superfine sugar
1–2 tablespoons light cream

Put the raspberries in a blender or food processor, then push through a fine nylon sieve or a fine vegetable mill to catch the seeds. If you are not using a machine, the whole thing can be done with a food mill. Stir in the sugar and cream, and serve in a jug, with Frozen Strawberry Fool or Vanilla Ice Cream.

Remember to remove the seeds when there are elderly people among your guests

Melted Milky Way Sauce

Serves 1–2
1 Milky Way bar
1 tablespoon half-and-half or light cream

Cut the Milky Way bar in pieces and melt, with the half-and-half or cream in a small pan over gentle heat. Stir, once melted, until smooth. Serve over Vanilla Ice Cream, when it will harden into a chocolate caramel shell. Enough for only 1–2 (it melts down surprisingly small). The worst part about this recipe is cleaning the pan afterward. Be careful not to pour any down the drain, or it may harden and block it up.

Do remember that kitchen knives can be very sharp

Oh My! Toffee Sauce

Serves 4
4 tablespoons (60 ml) syrup
4 tablespoons (60 g) soft brown sugar
2 tablespoons (30 ml) heavy cream (or more)

Put the syrup and sugar in a small pan and heat over medium heat. Bring to a boil and continue boiling until the mixture starts to thicken. Add the cream, and boil up once more. If too thick, add a little more cream. Serve hot, over Vanilla Ice Cream.

Hot Chocolate Sauce

Chocolate becomes lumpy if it is overheated

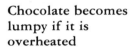

Serves 5–6
3½ ounces (100 g) dark chocolate
1 teaspoon instant coffee
⅔ cup (160 ml) boiling water
2 teaspoons superfine sugar
⅔ cup (160 ml) heavy cream

Break the chocolate in small bits and put it in a small saucepan. Dissolve the instant coffee in the boiling water and add to the chocolate. Heat gently, and cook over very low heat until the chocolate has melted. Add the sugar, stir until melted, then pour the cream in. Stir until blended and reheated, then pour into a heated jug or sauce boat and serve with Vanilla Ice Cream.

"Now, sit down at that table—there's stacks of letter-paper on it, with 'Toad Hall' at the top in blue and gold—and write invitations to all our friends, and if you stick to it we shall get them out before luncheon!"

Drop Cookies

Makes about 30

6 tablespoons (90 g) butter	1 egg, beaten
6 tablespoons (90 g) superfine sugar	1½ cups (175 g) self-rising flour
4 tablespoons (60 g) soft brown sugar	A pinch of salt

The baking sheets should be taken out and prepared before you start

Preheat the oven to 375° F (190° C). Cream the butter in a bowl, add the superfine sugar and cream again, then add the brown sugar and cream again. When all is smooth and well blended, add the beaten egg and stir well. Sift the flour with the salt and stir in. (All this can be done in the food processor, if convenient.) Have 2 or 3 cookie sheets, lightly oiled. Using 2 teaspoons, drop blobs of the mixture onto the sheets, leaving about 1¼ inches (3 cm) between them, as they will spread. It doesn't really matter if they run into each other, since they can be broken apart on cooling. Bake for about 12 minutes. When they are golden brown, darkening slightly around the edges, take the sheets out of the oven and cool for about 3 minutes, then lift off the cookies with a spatula. If they have run together, this is the time to separate them. Lay them on a rack to cool, when they will become very crisp. If you have only 1 cookie sheet they will take a little longer, as you will have to do them in three batches. Any that are not eaten the same day should be stored in a jar. Serve with ice cream, a fruit fool, or for tea.

"In due time," said the third, "we shall be home-sick once more for quiet water-lilies swaying on the surface of an English stream. But today all that seems pale and thin and very far away. Just now our blood dances to other music."

108

Bottled Sunshine Orange Cakes

Be sure to use
oven gloves or
potholders when
handling hot pans

Makes about 10
8 tablespoons (120 g) butter
½ cup (120 g) superfine sugar
Zest of 1 small orange
3 tablespoons orange juice
2 eggs
1 cup (120 g) all-purpose flour
A pinch of salt
Butter to grease pan

Preheat the oven to 375° F (190° C). Cream the butter, add the sugar, and cream again. Beat in the finely grated orange zest, then the juice. Break the eggs into a cup, beat, and stir into the butter mixture, then sift the flour with the salt and stir that in also. Have a muffin pan greased with butter, and put a blob of the mixture in each. Bake for about 15 minutes on the top shelf of the oven, or until they have risen to make a domed center that looks quite firm and set. Remove from the oven and leave for 2–3 minutes, then loosen the edges of the little cakes carefully with the point of a knife, lift them out, and set on a wire rack to cool. Serve the same day, with tea, or with a fruit fool or ice cream.

Soon they found some guava jelly in a glass dish, and a cold chicken, a tongue that had hardly been touched, some trifle, and quite a lot of lobster salad; and in the pantry they came upon a basketful of French rolls and any quantity of cheese, butter and celery.

Small Chocolate Cakes

Makes 6

½ teaspoon instant coffee

2 ounces (60 g) dark chocolate

6 tablespoons (90 g) butter

6 tablespoons (90 g) superfine sugar

¾ cup (90 g) all-purpose flour

1 large egg, beaten

Butter to grease pan

Preheat the oven to 375° F (190° C). Dissolve the instant coffee in 2 tablespoons boiling water in a small bowl. Break the chocolate into this and stand over a pan of simmering water until the chocolate has melted. Stir to blend with the coffee, and remove from the heat; leave to cool. Cream the butter, either by hand or in a food processor if you have one, add the sugar, and cream again until very well blended. Sift the flour and beat into the creamed butter, then add the beaten egg, and finally the (cooled) melted chocolate. Beat until smooth, then spoon into a six-cup muffin pan which you have greased with butter. Bake for about 15 minutes on the top shelf of the oven, until nicely risen. Turn out onto a wire rack to cool. Serve with cream as a dessert, or on their own with tea.

Do not open the oven door when baking until the cooking time is up. Cold air can make cakes and baked desserts collapse

" . . . patches of mud that smell like plum cake."
"The river . . . It's my world, and I don't want any other."

Plum Cake

A suitable pan
should be taken out
and prepared
before starting

½ pound (225 g) unsalted (sweet) butter
1 cup (225 g) soft brown sugar
2 tablespoons dark molasses
3 cups (350 g) self-rising flour
4 eggs
1½ teaspoons ground cloves
1½ teaspoons ground cinnamon
1½ teaspoons ground nutmeg
1 cup (100 g) ground almonds
1¼ cups (225 g) currants
1¼ cups (225 g) raisins
1¼ cups (225 g) golden raisins
4–5 tablespoons milk
Juice of 1 orange

Preheat the oven to 325° F (160° C). Take the butter out
of the refrigerator 1 hour before starting. Prepare a large
round cake pan, or 2 smaller loaf pans, lining them with
buttered wax paper. Cream the butter in a large bowl, then
add the sugar gradually, continuing to beat with a wooden
spoon. Warm the molasses over hot water, then stir into
the mixture. Sift the flour into another bowl. Break 1 egg
at a time into a cup, beat with a fork, then stir into the
butter-sugar mixture. After each egg, fold in a spoonful or
two of sifted flour. When all 4 eggs are used up, mix the 3
spices into the remaining flour and fold in. Stir in the
ground almonds, currants, and raisins. Finally, stir in the
milk and orange juice. Spoon the mixture into the prepared
pan or pans, and bake on the center shelf of the oven,
allowing 3 hours for the large pan or 2½ hours for the 2
smaller pans. After the first hour, cover the pans with a
piece of aluminum foil to prevent the cakes from getting
too brown. When they are cooked, tip them out of their
pans onto a wire rack to cool. Wrap in aluminum foil to
store, or put in an airtight jar. They keep well, up to 6
weeks, so can be made well in advance.

Carrot Cake

Makes 1 cake (serves 8)
Butter to grease pan
1¼ cups (275 g) sugar
1 cup (240 ml) sunflower or
    peanut oil
3 eggs
1½ cups (175 g) all-purpose
    flour
1½ teaspoons baking powder
1½ teaspoons ground
    cinnamon
½ teaspoon ground cloves
½ teaspoon salt
½ pound (225 g) carrots,
    peeled or scraped and
    grated

½ cup (120 g) walnuts, finely
    chopped

Frosting:
1 (3-ounce/85 g) package
    cream cheese, at room
    temperature
3 tablespoons (45 g) unsalted
    (sweet) butter
3 tablespoons (45 ml) superfine
    or confectioner's sugar

Do remember to stick to either standard U.S. *or* metric measurements. The equivalent weights or volume measurements are not exact and have been rounded off to make the recipes easier to follow

Line a deep cake pan (7 inches by 3 inches [18 by 8 cm] deep) with buttered wax paper and preheat oven to 350° F (175° C). Put the sugar in a large bowl and add the oil, beating it in with a wooden spoon. Break in the eggs, 1 at a time, beating each in until it is blended. Have the flour sifted into a bowl with the baking powder, cinnamon, cloves, and salt. Add these, spoonful by spoonful, to the egg mixture, beating thoroughly. Finally stir in the grated carrots and the chopped nuts. Tip the cake mixture into the prepared pan. Bake in the oven for 1 hour and 10–20 minutes, or until the top jumps back when pressed down with a finger. Tip out of its pan onto a wire rack to cool, removing the paper. An hour or so later, make the frosting. Put the cream cheese in a bowl—I use Philadelphia—and beat it with the back of a wooden spoon until smooth and creamy. Add the butter at room temperature, cut into small bits, and mash into the cream cheese with the spoon.

When both are blended, shake in the sugar and beat until all is smooth. When the cake is completely cold, tip it right side up onto a plate and spread the frosting over the top, smoothing it with a round-ended knife or spatula. If making a day ahead, keep in the refrigerator. This cake can be eaten either as a dessert, or for tea.

Index

A

All-Bran loaf, 5
Apple and blackberry meringue, 98
    snow, 27
    with chocolate, 94

B

Baked bananas, 94
    eggs with cheese and ham, 7
Banana pudding (easy), 22
Bananas, baked, 94
    sliced, in orange gelatin, 35
Blackberry and apple meringue, 98
    jelly (By-ways), 50–51
Bread and butter pudding
        (millionaires'), 93
    eggy, 2
Bubble and squeak, 22
Buried strawberries, 102

C

Cake, carrot, 112
    plum, 111
    potato, 21
Cakes, chocolate (small), 110
    orange (Bottled Sunshine), 109
Carrot cake, 112
Cauliflower, egg and shrimp
        mayonnaise, 78
    gratin, 10–11
Cheese, fried sandwiches, 3
    macaroni, 14
Cheesecake, 95
Chicken, broiled (River-bankers'),
        83
    noodle soup, 30–31

    pie, 84–85
Chocolate, apple with, 94
    cakes (small), 110
    chip cookies, 55
    sauce (hot), 107
Chutney, tomato, 49
Cinnamon toast, 4
Cod, smoked with tomatoes, 18
Cookies, chocolate chip, 55
    drop cookies, 108
    refrigerator, 56–57
Cornish pasties, 67
Crab apple jelly, 52
Crumble, plum, 98

D

Dark woods, snowfalls in, 92
Dipping sauce, 80
Drink, eggnog, 36
    honey and lemon, 38
    lemonade I, 39
    lemonade II, 39
    milk shake (ripple), 36

E

Eggnog, 36
Egg salad, 9
Eggs, baked with cheese and ham,
        7
    curried, 8
    hard-cooked, with nutty spice
        island mixture, 63
    in onion sauce, 79
    scrambled with tomato puree, 6
    stuffed, 62
Eggy bread, 2

F

Fish cakes, salmon, 90
    pie, 15
    potted, 42
Flapjacks, 75
    very easy, 74
Floating islands, 100
Fried cheese sandwiches, 3
    marmalade sandwiches, 2
Frozen Milky Way, 54
    strawberry fool, 101
Fruit fool, mixed, 23

G

Game pie, 88–89
Gelatin, orange, with sliced
    bananas, 35
Gratin, cauliflower, 10–11

H

Haddock, smoked, with tomatoes,
    18
Ham, boiled with parsley sauce, 20
Herrings in oatmeal, 17
Honey and lemon drink, 38
Hot meat pasties, 68–69

I

Ice cream, nut grove, 104–05
    vanilla, 102
Islands, floating, 100

J

Jam, blackberry (By-ways), 50–51
    plum, 54
    roly-poly, 26
Jelly, crab apple, 52

K

Kedgeree, 16–17
Kipper paste, 45

L

Leek pudding, 19
Lemonade, 39
Lemon and honey drink, 38
Lettuce snacks (Leafy Summer), 66
Loaf, All-Bran, 5

M

Macaroni cheese, 14
Marmalade sandwiches, fried, 2
Marmite soldiers (Moly's), 33
Milky Way, frozen, 54
    melted, sauce, 106
Mayonnaise, cauliflower, egg and
    shrimp, 78
Meat loaf (easy), 72
Meringue, apple and blackberry,
    98
Milk shake (ripple), 36
Mixed fruit fool, 23
Mushrooms on toast, 4

N

Nut grove ice cream, 104–05
Nutty spice island mixture, 48
    eggs with, 63

O

Onion sauce, 79
Onions, pickled, 47

P

Pancakes, 24–25
Parsley sauce, 20
Paste, kipper, 45
Pasties, Cornish, 67
    hot meat, 68–69
    rabbit, 70–71
Pearly dawn sorbet, 103
Pebbles in a stream, 99
Pickled onions, 47
Pie, chicken, 84–85
    fish, 15
    game, 88–89
    steak and kidney, 86–87
Pizza (Wayfarers' easy), 12–13
Plum cake, 111
    crumble, 98
    jam, 54
Potato cake, 21
    puree, 91
    soup, 32
Potted fish, 43
    meat (Ratty's), 42
    shrimp (Marseilles), 46

shrimp sandwich, 61
Pudding, banana (easy), 22
   bread and butter (millionaires'),
     93
   leek, 19
   rice (simple), 34

R
Rabbit pasties, 70–71
Raw vegetables with dipping sauce,
   80
Refrigerator cookies, 56–57
Rice pudding (simple), 34
River-bankers' lunch, 62
Riverside sandwich, 60

S
Salad, egg, 9
Salmon fish cakes, 90
Sandwiches, fried cheese, 3
   fried marmalade, 2
   Moly's Marmite soldiers, 33
   potted shrimp, 61
   riverside, 60
   sausage, 60
   steak (Toad Hall), 61
Sardines on toast, 3
Sauce, barbecue, 82–83
   chocolate (hot), 107
   dipping, 80
   melted Milky Way, 106
   onion, 79
   parsley, 20
   raspberry, 106
   toffee (Oh My!), 107
Sausage rolls, 64–65
   sandwich, 60
Scrambled eggs with tomato puree,
   6

Shrimp, Marseilles potted, 46
   sandwich, 61
Smoked haddock (or cod) with
   tomatoes, 18
Snowfalls in dark woods, 92
Sorbet, pearly dawn, 103
Soup, chicken noodle, 30–31
   potato, 32
Spare Ribs (Red Lion) with
   barbecue sauce, 82–83
Spice mixture (nutty spice island),
   48
Steak and kidney pie, 86–87
   sandwich (Toad Hall), 61
Strawberries, buried, 102
Strawberry fool, frozen, 101
Stroganoff, veal, 81
Stuffed eggs, 62

T
Toad-in-a-bad-hole, 11
Toast, cinnamon, 4
   mushrooms on, 4
   sardines on, 3
Toffee sauce (Oh My!), 107
Tomato chutney, 49
Trifle (Toad Hall), 96–97

V
Vanilla ice cream, 102
Veal stroganoff, 81
Vegetables, raw, with dipping
   sauce, 80

W
Wayfarers' easy pizza, 12–13